About the Author

I am a true believer in communicating with the Universe. Since I truly believe it, I decided to write about how the Universe hears wishes only your heart can make. Many of the characters in my book are based on people who played a significant part in my life. Some are no longer with us, and some still are.

I have two wonderful sons, Nicolaos and Christopher, for whom I love to cook. I also have two beautiful cats, Hermes and Electra. I love to watch hockey; the New York Rangers are my favorite team.

Angels Deployed

Sophia Pavlou

Angels Deployed

VANGUARD PAPERBACK

© Copyright 2024
Sophia Pavlou

The right of Sophia Pavlou to be identified as author of this work has been asserted by her in accordance with the Copyright, Designs and Patents Act 1988.

All Rights Reserved

No reproduction, copy or transmission of this publication may be made without written permission.
No paragraph of this publication may be reproduced, copied or transmitted save with the written permission of the publisher, or in accordance with the provisions of the Copyright Act 1956 (as amended).

Any person who commits any unauthorised act in relation to this publication may be liable to criminal prosecution and civil claims for damages.

A CIP catalogue record for this title is available from the British Library.

ISBN 978-1-80016-759-9

This is a work of fiction. Names, characters, businesses, places, events and incidents are either the products of the author's imagination or used in a fictitious manner. Any resemblance to actual persons, living or dead, or actual events is purely coincidental.

*Vanguard Press is an imprint of
Pegasus Elliot Mackenzie Publishers Ltd.*
www.pegasuspublishers.com

First Published in 2024

**Vanguard Press
Sheraton House Castle Park
Cambridge England**

Printed & Bound in Great Britain

Chapter 1

It's a weird and wonderful thing living in a town surrounded by water. One enjoys the cooling sea breeze during the summertime and biting, freezing wind in the winter. There are beautiful sunsets of orange and pink as the sun says good night, its work complete for the day, and the brilliant moon lights up the night sky, offering a million stars to wish upon.

The weather in Watchtower Harbor can be as predictably unpredictable as a child who swears they want chocolate ice cream when their parents know vanilla is their favorite. They will change their mind after the ice cream is ordered. Perhaps that's why the locals carry umbrellas wherever they go and have raincoats in the back seats of their cars. They know the blue skies can quickly and unexpectedly turn to gray.

Watchtower Harbor is not unlike any other small seaside fishing town. The locals are friendly to the tourists who vacation here year after year. The locals know that their town would be swallowed by horrible strip malls and box stores like Lowe's and Best Buy without tourists. The tourists come to get away from their hectic big-city lives and enjoy being taken back to a time of innocence and purity, a time when a person's word and a handshake meant something, and strangers returned a smile with a nod of the head or a tip of the cap. Ceramic flower pots filled with red-and-white double geraniums line Main Street on perfectly spaced sidewalks, and people actually use the crosswalks.

One of the most popular places in town is Nick's General Store. Established in 1870, it has creaky floors, and wooden barrels that once held sugar and flour, and a scale hangs from the ceiling. Nick, a pleasant Greek man, came to Watchtower in the early 1970s after serving in the United States Army. He weighs out gumdrops, licorice, and salt water taffy for the visitors and sightseers who love to come in and get a feel for small-town America. He wears a white apron the way proprietors did in days gone by. He always has a smile for his customers, whether they live there or come for vacation. When parents aren't looking, he sneaks a piece of salt water taffy into the hands of children. Some say he has a soft spot for the little ones.

Julia and Sophie are his favorite little girls. They live in Watchtower Harbor with their parents, Annalise and Sean. The girls go to the general store a couple of times a week after school with their mom to get ice cream, candy, or something to drink. Sean is in the Navy and deployed for long periods of time. Nick adores the girls and spoils them the way a grandfather would. Out of respect for his age, the girls call him Grandpa Nick. He can't quite put his finger on it; he just knows something is special about the girls. He and their dad have a bond only people who have served in the military know.

As you leave the general store and walk down Main Street, you will hear booming, bonging sounds from the belfry of the Greek Orthodox church in the center of town. Across the street from the church is the Town Hall, which people come in and out of all day: contractors getting permits for upcoming work, locals paying their taxes or a parking ticket they swear they didn't deserve just because they parked in the FIRE ZONE in front of the thrift shop to drop off old, useless items that other people might want to buy. Down Main Street is the town pier, where fishermen dock their boats to unload freshly caught lobsters, clams, and oysters that will end up on the dinner menu of various local restaurants. In addition to the commercial fishing boats, sailboats, cabin cruisers, sloops, and a houseboat dock there. It must be two p.m.: there goes the blast of the ferry's foghorn. The ferry runs three times a day during the summer months, bringing more tourists from the city for the day or the weekend. Watchtower Harbor is a quick getaway for people living in the city who want to leave behind the stress of their everyday lives. They vow that one day they will give up the craziness and move to Watchtower to enjoy a simpler life.

Chapter 2
The Beach

The tide was vigorous, one wave after another rolling in, rushing towards the dunes. Sophie was busy building her sandcastle, thinking of a different design than she had yesterday. Julia, Sophie's bossy older sister, told her not to build her castle so close to the water, to move closer to the dunes; that way, when the tide came in, her castle would last a little longer and not be washed away. Sophie, being the headstrong four-year-old, paid little attention to what Julia was saying. She wasn't going to be pushed around or told what to do just because Julia was older.

The girls loved having their own private beach. Their house was beachfront with a wooden staircase that led down to the water, so their mom could keep a close eye on them. They played almost every day after school when the warm weather started.

Once again, Julia tried to tell Sophie her castle would be washed away and look like a lump of sand that no one wanted to see.

"You think you know more than I do because you are in second grade," Sophie said. "Besides, Daddy is here, and he is going to keep the water from wrecking my castles."

Julia had a puzzled look on her face.

"What are you talking about?" she said. "Daddy is away."

"No, he isn't," Sophie said, stomping her foot on the sand. "Daddy is right there in the water."

"That's not Daddy," exclaimed Julia. "That's a seal."

"Mommy said Daddy is a seal."

"Not that kind of seal," said Julia. "That's what Daddy's work is and the way he swims."

Being four-years-old, Sophie had a very active imagination. She thought when her father went away for work, he didn't really go anywhere but turned himself into a seal and would watch her and her sister play on the beach.

"You believe what you want, and I believe what I want," Sophie said. "Stop being such a bossy pants, Julia, or that will be your new nickname. Julia Bossy Pants."

Their mother was calling them. Time for them to pack up and go inside. Sophie gathered up her sandcastle molds and shovel and put them in her backpack. She wiped the sand off her favorite dolly, put the dolly in her backpack's middle pocket, and started walking towards the stairs. Julia packed her backpack, putting her stuffed animals in carefully to make sure there was room for all of them. She double-checked the front pocket to make sure the picture of her father was there. Julia always carried a picture of her father. If she or her sister missed him, they would look at the picture, and he wouldn't seem so far away. Even though she and Sophie argued most of the day and Sophie got on Julia's nerves, Julia was always the first person to comfort Sophie when she started missing their father.

The girls had a ritual before going into the house. They washed the sand off their legs and feet in the outdoor shower then stopped in their playhouse to eat the snack their mom had made for them. They talked about what they were going to do and what they were going to play once they went into the house.

Chapter 3
Harrisburg, Pennsylvania

In Ralph Waldo Emerson Elementary School in Harrisburg, Ms Beck's third-grade class had just finished the Pledge of Allegiance and was settling in to start the day. Every morning, she had the class take a moment and send a positive thought for a friend or family member who was far away.

One of Ms Beck's more outgoing and funnier students, Jimmy Andrews, always sent the same message to his much older brother Scott, or "Scooter," as he was known to his friends. Scott was Jimmy's half-brother. They had the same father but a different mother. Their father had remarried a few years after Scott's mother died.

Jimmy idolized Scott; he planned on joining the Army and becoming a helicopter pilot just like his older brother. Since Scooter's deployment, he was the only thing on Jimmy's mind. Jimmy was missing Scott a great deal; Jimmy couldn't seem to concentrate on the two things he loved most: making his friends laugh and writing. According to Ms Beck, Jimmy excelled at writing. But he wasn't going near his journal at snack time or during indoor recess. She wondered if something was bothering him. She wanted to ask him if everything was all right, but

Jimmy was a proud child, and she had to be careful about approaching him without embarrassing him.

As luck would have it, today it was raining, so after lunch, recess would be in the gym. The kids didn't mind indoor recess; at times, they seemed to prefer it. The gym was equipped with basketball hoops and nets for either volleyball or badminton, whatever the kids felt like playing. If they wanted to play by themselves, there were jump ropes, the good kind made from leather that created a whipping sound when they went around and a slapping sound when they hit the ground, not the cheap plastic ones that got tangled and twisted before you got a chance to go around once. The only sound those made was the frustrated grunts from the students using them.

Jimmy was a private kid and never spoke about himself or said if something was bothering him, but **Ms Beck** had thought of a plan to try and get him to open up and talk about what was on his mind without asking him in front of his classmates. She told her class she would pick a student's name out of a bowl to see who would be the lucky one and have lunch with her in the classroom rather than the cafeteria. To try and make things look fair and square without the kids realizing she was rigging the game, she handed out colored strips of paper for the kids to write their names on. Jimmy's strip of paper was a slightly different color, a darker green than the strips she gave the other students, so she would know which one was his.

"All right," Jimmy said. "I got the Army green one."

The kids in the class couldn't believe it. All he ever talked about was the Army, so they told him it was his lucky day. Ms Beck's plan was going to work as far as she was concerned. They'd noticed the different color, but none of them suspected anything.

She told her class to finish up the math problem they were working on and not to worry if they hadn't completed their worksheet. After lunch, before they went to the library, they would have time to finish it. Lunchtime was approaching, and she needed to pick out the name of the lucky student who would have lunch with her. The kids finished their work, shoved their papers inside their desks, and waited for Ms Beck to call out a name. As she reached into the fish bowl, she reminded the kids that if they didn't get called this time, she would do this again, and someone else would get a chance in a couple of weeks. She didn't want to hear any of the moaning or groaning that comes out of the mouths of third graders when they don't get what they want. Her hand was in the fishbowl, but she was already holding Jimmy's paper. She had put it there when the kids were working on their math. She made sure to twirl her hand in the bowl to make it look like she was mixing up all the papers. She hated deceiving her students, but this was for a good reason. She needed Jimmy to open up and talk about what was bothering him.

When Jimmy heard his name, he wasn't thrilled; the last thing he wanted to do was sit and have lunch with his teacher. She was friendly. He liked her, but would much rather have lunch in the cafeteria with everyone else. Then again, he wasn't in the mood to go to the gym. So, he would make the best of having lunch in his classroom.

As the kids shuffled to get in line, Ms Beck heard the usual complaints about how Jack wasn't in the correct order or how Tina, the line leader, kept flipping her hair and annoying everyone behind her. The way she flipped her hair, you would think she was the second coming of Cher. Ms Beck wasn't surprised Tina didn't have many friends. Ms Beck told Jimmy to wait in the classroom at his desk until she returned from taking the kids to the lunchroom.

When Ms Beck got back, Jimmy hadn't started eating yet. "Thank you for waiting," Ms Beck said.

"Well, we are supposed to eat lunch together," Jimmy said. "If I started without you, it really wouldn't be together."

She asked him if he would like to join her at the back table, where she usually corrected the kids' work. He grabbed his lunch box and headed towards the back. He sat down in the chair, unpacked his lunch, and started to eat.

"What do you have for lunch?" asked Ms Beck.

"Ham on white bread with mayonnaise. It's Scott's favorite. He makes lunch for us when he is home. After we eat, we play video games."

Since Jimmy had mentioned Scott's name, Ms Beck knew it might be her only chance to get Jimmy to talk about his brother. She was positive Scott being deployed was what was bothering Jimmy. When she was little, Matt, her older brother, had been deployed, and she still remembered how sad and quiet she had become. She never felt like talking to anyone either.

"Oh yeah?" she said. "What kind of games do you play?" She hoped Jimmy would respond with something more than a shrug.

"It depends," he said. "Sometimes, we play with the flight simulator. You know where you pretend to be flying, but you really aren't. Sometimes we play a racing car simulator, and we race around real NASCAR tracks. His favorite track is Dover. It's a short track. They can't go very fast. I like the superspeedways. My favorite is Pocono. The cars go really fast. We usually play on both tracks, so it's fair to both of us. I think he lets me win, even though he says he doesn't."

Ms Beck saw the sadness creeping across Jimmy's face again. She was getting used to that look, and she didn't want to see it on his face, or on any of her other students' faces, for that matter. She might have changed the subject, but she didn't. If she did, she might never get another chance to talk about Scott. "When was the last time you were able to talk to Scott or email him?"

"I can email him any time," Jimmy said. "He responds when he can. Sometimes, when he does, he gives me a day and time that we might be able to Skype if the signal is strong enough."

"You know there is another way of getting a message to Scott," Ms Beck said. Jimmy looked puzzled.

"How?" Jimmy asked. "Scott would tease me about sending smoke signals, but we know that would never work because I'm not allowed to go near matches, and I don't know how to start a fire."

Ms Beck laughed. "Your brother is hilarious, but that's not what I was thinking."

Jimmy continued to look at her. What was she talking about? How else could you send a message other than an email or phone call?

"How?" He was dying to find out what she was talking about. If he could, Jimmy would Skype with Scott every day, not just when the signal was strong enough.

Ms Beck walked over to her supply cabinet and took out a big bag of barbeque potato chips, the good kind that looked like waffles, not the regular, thin chips that were always broken into pieces in the bag. The waffle ones were crunchier than the normal, boring ones. She grabbed two napkins, opened them up, and poured the chips onto them, one pile of chips for her, one for Jimmy.

Ms Beck was trying to gauge Jimmy's interest in what she was saying and whether to continue talking about her unusual way of contacting Scott. Jimmy was crunching away on his chips when she started talking again.

"Jimmy, on your birthday, before you blow out the candles on your cake, you make a wish, correct?"

"You bet I do. This year you know what I am going to wish for?"

"Don't tell me, or it won't come true," she reminded him.

"You're right. Thanks for stopping me, Ms Beck."

"Did you ever wish when it wasn't your birthday for Scott to contact you?" she asked.

"No," Jimmy said, "wishes are only for birthdays or Christmas."

"Not always."

People make wishes in all kinds of other ways. People wish upon stars, throw coins into wishing wells, or blow on dandelions. But if she brought up all those things, she might lose Jimmy's attention and not have a chance to talk about what she really wanted to talk about.

"Sometimes," she said, "we want something so badly, our hearts make wishes for us, even when it's not our birthday or Christmas. Like now, I know you are missing Scott. You miss him so much, your heart is sending out messages to the wind, and you don't even know it. The wind takes it to special angels that are like messengers that somehow bring the messages to him or anyone we miss very much."

Jimmy looked at his teacher as if she had lost her mind. How can your heart send out messages? It can't think. Only your brain can make wishes. He really liked Ms Beck and would never say anything to hurt her feelings, but part of him thought she was cuckoo for Cocoa Puffs. On the other hand, he was miserable, so why not hear what Ms Beck had to say? He was embarrassed to ask the next question but did it anyway.

"Ms Beck, I'm not sure what you are talking about. But I really miss Scott a lot. If you tell me what to do, I just might try it."

Ms Beck truly believed that angels made wishes come true. She was relieved and happy that Jimmy wanted to hear what she had to say. She had seen the look on his face and realized he must think she was crazy. But she wanted to share her experience with him because she understood his sadness firsthand.

"Of course, it's really very simple," Ms Beck said. "Go somewhere where it's quiet and think about Scott. Say either to yourself or out loud the first thing that comes to your mind about Scott because it's really what your heart is feeling."

When she was little and her brother had been deployed to Bosnia, her wish had come true. She had wished so hard that he would contact her soon, he did the very next day. Of course, one could say that was purely coincidental, but Ms Beck knew her wish had been heard and answered by the angels in the wind.

"I am going to get the class from lunch," she said. "That will give you a few minutes alone to think about what you want Scott to hear and send it out into the wind."

Jimmy went over by the window. Even though it was still raining, he opened it; he didn't want to take any chances of his message being blocked. He thought long and hard and knew he had to make it fast because the class was on its way back. He closed his eyes.

"I feel really silly doing this. Hi out there in the universe, clouds, or space. My name is Jimmy Andrews. I am eight-years-old. I live in Harrisburg, Pennsylvania. My brother Scott is a sergeant in the Army. He is a part of the Air Cavalry Unit, and he is in Afghanistan. He goes on a lot of missions. I haven't heard from him in like two months. Can you please tell him to email me when he can? I'm kinda scared he is hurt. Thanks, Jimmy Andrews."

Just then, all the kids entered the room, and things were back to normal as far as Jimmy was concerned. As silly as he felt a minute ago, something made him feel better. He wasn't so sad any more.

Chapter 4
The Girls' House

Annalise, the girls' mother, radiated both inner and outer beauty. Her flaxen blonde hair shined even on the gloomiest of days, and her eyes were bluer than the sky. Her smile lit up a room like a thousand candles during a power failure. No matter how much she worried about her husband and the danger he was in with every mission he went on, she continued to smile and stay positive for the girls' sake.

She was aware of her girls' unique ability to hear messages from children whose family members were deployed and channel them to the soldiers. The girls understood what it was like to miss someone when they were deployed because of their father. As a result, they had been chosen to be messengers by a higher being. Annalise wasn't a hundred percent sure, but that must have been the main reason. Perhaps there was another reason they were chosen. Once upon a time, she'd been chosen, too.

When the girls were younger, they still didn't understand how extraordinary their gift was; they probably didn't even understand they had a gift. They may have thought that all little girls and boys could hear wishes and answer them. One day when Julia was six- years-old, Annalise had heard her daughter talking to herself.

Annalise listened in on what Julia was saying. Perhaps she was playing make-believe. But no, it wasn't make-believe; this was a wish coming through. Annalise could tell because of Julia's conversation, and the location Julia mentioned was real. At that point, Annalise explained to Julia that not every little boy or girl in the world could hear wishes and just how very special Julia and her sister were. Out of all the boys and girls in the world, they had been chosen to help the family members of soldiers by carrying messages to moms, dads, brothers, and sisters when they couldn't talk or email. Sophie was only three, and she was in the room with them, listening to what her mom was saying. Sophie was a little too young to understand. Now she was a year older and had seen what happened with Julia, and she understood what was happening because it had happened to her not long after she turned four.

This afternoon wasn't any different than any other day. The girls were sitting on the patio waiting for their mom to finish making their lunches. They ate the same thing all the time, ham on white bread with the crust cut off, cut in the shape of sailboats. Annalise asked if they wanted potato chips. They both said yes. She asked them if they wanted yucky or regular chips. Yucky—or salt and vinegar—chips got their name because the first time the girls tried them, the first words that came out of their mouths were, "These are yucky, Mommy, throw them out. They are gross." In time, however, they became Julia's favorite.

"Yucky chips for me, please," Julia yelled from outside.

"Not me. I hate them. Barbeque is my favorite," said Sophie.

They didn't have barbeque. Sophie was not happy with either of their choices and let her mother know it.

"How come you always get Julia her favorite chips but never mine?"

"Because I'm the oldest and Mommy's favorite!"

"No, you're not."

"Oh yes I am. She always buys my favorite chips and never yours, so that proves it."

"Girls, girls, you are both my favorites in different ways. I stopped in the general store. Grandpa Nick said he was waiting for his potato chip delivery later today. So I bought what was on the rack." Annalise was hoping not to have a screaming match on her hands before lunch.

Within minutes of Annalise giving the girls their lunch, Julia got a faraway look in her eyes. Annalise and Sophie knew what that meant. Neither of them said anything to her for fear of interrupting her and not having the message pass on to her properly. A few minutes later, Julia snapped out of her daydream and asked Sophie if she heard the wish.

"No, I didn't," Sophie said. "I'm sorry, I was eating."

"What did you hear, darling?" their mom asked.

"It was a boy. He said: 'Hi out there in the universe, clouds, or space. My name is Jimmy Andrews. I am eight-years-old. I live in Harrisburg, Pennsylvania. My brother Scott is a sergeant in the Army. He is a part of the Air Cavalry Unit, and he is in Afghanistan. He goes on a lot of missions. I haven't heard from him in like two months. Can you please tell him to email me when he can? I'm kinda scared he is hurt. Thanks, Jimmy Andrews.'

"Mommy, he is only a year older than I am," said Julia.

"That's right, sweetheart, he is."

"He must miss his brother the way we miss Daddy when he is away."

"I am sure he does," Annalise said.

"Where is Harrisburg, Pennsylvania?"

"It's a state not too far from where we live," Annalise said. "Let me show you on the map."

The three of them went into the family room. Two maps were taped to the back wall, one of the United States and the other of the rest of the world. When their father came home from a mission or the girls received a wish, Annalise would mark the maps by putting a pushpin in them to show the girls where states or countries were located. She saw this as a teachable moment in geography for the girls. Even though they were young, their mother took any opportunity to teach the girls something new, such as where countries were.

Annalise sat down on the little wooden chair that had come with the play table the girls sat at when they wanted to draw, color, or play with their Lego sets. Now that Legos came in pink and purple, Julia enjoyed playing with them even more because those were supposed to be girls' colors. Sophie, on the other hand, had always liked building with Legos. She didn't care what color they were.

Annalise took a pushpin out of the sealed container and started to show the girls exactly where Harrisburg was.

It was the capital of Pennsylvania; she put the pin right on the star. The girls showed their mom where Afghanistan was. Because, as Sophie pointed out, their father had been deployed there for six months, but it felt more like six years since she missed him so much.

The geography lesson was over. Annalise went outside to clean up the chips and cups still on the table. She went into the kitchen, loaded up the dishwasher, and cleaned up. She knew Julia needed a little quiet time to concentrate on where Scott was and to be able to relay Jimmy's message.

At times Sophie got messages, too. However, she was still a little too young to truly grasp what happened to her and what to do with it. She got a tingly feeling along with a faraway look whenever someone was trying to communicate with her. When that happened, Annalise grabbed a pencil and started writing everything down, just as she did with Julia.

Julia didn't feel like coloring. She wanted to contact Scott. She knew it was important to Jimmy for her to do that as soon as she could. She went outside and sat under her favorite tree, a giant oak. With its big green leaves, it provided shade to most of the backyard. She leaned against the tree trunk and focused on Jimmy's message and where on the map Scott was.

Chapter 5
Kandahar, Afghanistan

Scooter and his co-pilot gunner, Trevor Greenhill, geared up for another night flight scouting mission. Lt. Colonel Michael Cullen of Central Command in Kandahar had received orders from the bigwigs in Washington to go and check a grain warehouse on the outskirts of Kabul, about three hundred miles north of where they were stationed. The warehouse, Mike was told, was a bunker where the extremists were hiding underground, possibly plotting their next location to blow up, or it could be an actual grain warehouse. They had to check out every bit of information they received.

The men, especially Scooter, respected Mike as an officer and loved him as a person. Scooter and Mike had worked together for more than ten years and become as close as family. Scooter respected many things about Mike, but one thing especially. He never wanted his men to call him by his rank. He was Mike. As he rose through the chain of command, he always stayed humble, "one of the boys," and never acted like the officers Scooter hated.

It was 0000 hours (midnight). Along with Scooter and Trevor, their team consisted of two more pilots and two more co-pilot gunners, for a total of three helicopters. They would fly at 0100 hours. Scooter made sure everyone did yet another entire pre-flight inspection safety check. Scooter was a stickler for safety.

"Don't tell me, let me guess: pre-flight inspection," said Trevor

"You bet! Since you and this bird are my responsibility, we don't go up until I say we go."

"Thanks, Dad!"

"Trevor, it is an honor and a privilege to fly this bird. I'm gonna take care of it like my own baby. you will thank me one day for making sure I kept your sorry butt safe."

Trevor had been Scooter's co-pilot for four years. For the past three years, he had dreaded all the safety checks Scooter made them do. But he also appreciated the fact Scooter was such a stickler and probably would never trust anyone to fly with as much as he trusted Scooter.

The safety check completed, they climbed into the helicopter. Given that they were scouts, many of their missions were flying at night, hoping to go undetected by extremists. Since they knew where they were flying this time, they didn't think they would encounter any enemy fire. Nevertheless, if they did, they would be ready to fire back.

According to Scooter, tonight should be relatively easy. Go up, fly three hundred miles, take a look at the structure, which might or might not be a radar site, an underground bunker, or a grain warehouse, take some notes, and be back by 0600. Since it was supposed to be a warehouse, there shouldn't be much movement around there in the middle of the night. The team had orders to destroy the building if it looked as if it were being used to store military equipment. If they had any other problem, Apaches were well equipped to blow things up or shoot things down.

"Here we go," said Scooter. A surge of adrenaline coursed through his veins when the click, click, click of the switches on the control panel changed from the off position to on. Seconds later, the humming of the rotor blades started as they went around and around counterclockwise, moving the air over them. Lift-off! The Apaches took off swiftly, getting into position behind Scooter and Trevor. They were first in line. They were in a staggered position, making sure to give each helicopter enough room to fly safely without hitting the blades of another helicopter. It would have been catastrophic if the blades of the helicopters touched. The explosion would be disastrous; the loss of life would be tragic.

Apaches were also known to fly low to the ground. Tonight wouldn't be any different. They would be flying about one hundred feet in the air, so as not to be detected by enemy radar—a total blackout on navigation lights, along with radio silence between the pilots and home base.

After two and a half hours, they reached their destination. They were approximately three miles from the warehouse, according to their onboard display screens. They were careful not to get too much closer; if something was happening on the ground, they might be heard, initiating a firefight. If a fight broke out, they were well prepared for it, but they would rather that didn't happen. Communications between the helicopters were switched back on so the pilots could discuss their plans. The team stayed for twenty-five minutes. Boxes and crates were being moved from trucks into the warehouse. They agreed to head back to base, report what they had seen to Mike, and decide their next move.

They landed at approximately 0545, a little earlier than Scooter had thought they would. They were flying with the wind and it bought them time. They were exhausted and headed straight to bed for some well-deserved sleep, except for Scooter, being the senior member of the team and the one who needed to report back to Mike. He was hoping the conversation would not last too long. He wanted to go to bed, too.

Scooter went to Mike's office, where Mike was anxiously waiting for his men to come back safely. Mike had stayed awake the entire time the team was away. No way would he be able to sleep while he had six of his men on a scouting mission.

"How did it go?" asked Mike.

"All quiet on the western front," replied Scooter.

"For a pilot, you have a lousy sense of direction. We are in the Middle East."

"Okay, fine, all quiet on the Middle Eastern front."

"That's what I need, a wisenheimer at 0600. Now, seriously tell me what you saw so we both can get some sleep."

"Nothing too crazy to report, but we did see men moving boxes from trucks into a warehouse. I want to go back, if not tonight, definitely tomorrow. We can never be too sure," Scooter said.

Mike nodded in agreement. "Go and get some sleep, Scooter."

"Good night, sir." Scooter said that to bother Mike, teasing him because he hated it when his men called him sir.

Mike gave Scott a "get out of my office, now" look. He knew Scott called him sir on purpose just to annoy him.

Scooter crawled onto his bunk. "Home sweet home," he said. He thought he would fall asleep the second his head hit his pillow, but no such luck. He wasn't tossing or turning. He just couldn't get comfortable. He had finally drifted off when he woke up suddenly, from what he thought was a dream, but it all seemed too real. A beautiful little blonde girl was standing in front of him with a white light surrounding her. That made him sit straight up on his bunk.

The little girl spoke to him.

"Hi Scott, my name is Julia. My mother told me to tell you not to be afraid of me. People think they are seeing a ghost, but I'm not a ghost. I'm a special girl who is just a little different than other kids my age. I'm a messenger. I bring messages to soldiers that are away from kids in their families that really miss them. I have a message from Jimmy. He misses you very much and is worried you might have gotten hurt, and that's why you haven't contacted him. He really wants you to email him or call him or Skype with him as soon as you can."

Scooter didn't know what to think. Was he dreaming? Was he seeing things that weren't there? If so, that would be very bad for his flying career. A pilot can't see things that aren't there. He would lose his wings and get put out to pasture in the funny farm for sure. But he didn't give much thought to himself. He was more concerned about how this little girl knew Jimmy. Was Jimmy worried about him? It's true he hadn't written or Skyped with his little brother in quite a while. The guilt was eating at him every day. It wasn't because he didn't want to. It was because they had "no communication" orders until further notice. Scooter looked around and saw that Trevor was in his bunk, sound asleep. Scooter was pretty sure Trevor didn't see or hear the little girl.

At first, he thought it was just a dream, and he should try to go back to sleep. But he was worried about Jimmy and baffled about who Julia was and how she got there. He had questions but no answers, or none that made sense. The only thing Scooter knew was that despite the no-communication orders, he had to get permission and get in touch with Jimmy. He never went this long without talking to Jimmy. Scott tried to write to Jimmy at least once a week, but it had been two months, and he felt horrible. He needed to talk to Mike about it first, then figure out when would be a good time to call when Jimmy would still be home and not have left for school. Scooter was eight and a half hours ahead of Jimmy. Jimmy was an early bird, and if Scooter called at 0700 Harrisburg time, Jimmy would still be home. If it was 0700 in Pennsylvania, what time would it be in Afghanistan? Scooter wasn't going to be able to get back to sleep. He got up, dressed, and took a walk around the base. He couldn't put a clear thought together, so he asked some of the guys, who told him 0700 in Pennsylvania would be 1530 here. It was 0900 now. Plenty of time to talk to Mike and get him to pull the right strings for Scooter to make his phone call.

Scott had told Jimmy that if he didn't hear from Scott for a long time, it would mean he'd gotten hurt and couldn't get in touch with Jimmy. No one else would have known that Scott had said that but Jimmy. Even though Scott couldn't explain who Julia was, her message had to be from Jimmy.

Scooter grabbed two cups of coffee from the mess hall and headed to Mike's office.

"Hey Mike, you busy?" he asked.

"Not any more. I just got off the phone with Washington, briefing them on what you saw or didn't see last night. I told them you want to go again either tonight or tomorrow night, and they agreed, so whenever you want to go, it's your call."

"Roger that, I'll let you know," Scooter said.

"Okay, what's on your mind? You look perplexed. I have a funny feeling it's not about flying."

"Well, I am. I need your help, and you need to pull some strings."

"Oh boy, this could be interesting."

Scooter hardly ever asked for help from anyone. He believed he should always clean his own plate. If he ever asked Mike for help, Mike knew he had a good reason for asking.

"I need you to open up the lines so that I can get a quick call to Jimmy."

"Your little brother?" asked Mike.

"That's would be the one."

"Are you trying to get me thrown out of the Army? My retirement is coming up. I have a lake house in Louisiana I plan on going to and do nothing but fish all day, and you want me to let you make a call? Are you nuts? Who do you think I am to pull those kind strings? Geppetto?"

"Is that a yes?" asked Scooter.

Scooter knew he was asking a lot of Mike. When the directive came down from headquarters for no communications that was exactly what it meant: no communications, no contact, no nothing until the order was lifted.

"No promises."

"You are my favorite officer in the U.S. Army. I'll need to call him around 1530 local time."

"Get out of here before I change my mind," Mike said.

He and Scooter had been friends for many years. If Scooter needed to get in touch with Jimmy, whatever the reason, Mike knew it was important. He wasn't going to let Scooter down. He would figure out something. Mike owed a lot to Scooter. When Mike's son was young, he was in a car accident, and he lost a lot of blood due to a head injury. Scooter was the same blood type as Mike's son. As much as Scooter hated needles, he didn't hesitate to donate blood to the hospital blood bank. Mike was convinced his son lived and made a full recovery because of Scooter. From that point on, Mike felt indebted to Scooter. Though Scooter never wanted that subject brought up again; he thought he'd done what he needed to do, and Mike didn't owe him anything.

When 1530 finally came, Scooter headed over to Mike's office.

"You can have five minutes. You better make the call quick," said Mike.

"You bet."

Scooter had to remember how to make a call to the United States. No matter how many times he called, he couldn't remember. He could remember the exact date and time when he first piloted a helicopter, but he couldn't remember how to call home. He did okay, and the phone started ringing. Now he hoped Jimmy was awake and would answer the phone.

"Hello."

"Hey buddy," said Scooter.

"Scott, is that you? Mom, come quick, it's Scott," Jimmy yelled.

"I don't have a lot of time, buddy. How are you doing?"

"I'm doing okay. I was really worried about you, so my teacher told me to talk to the universe to send you a message that I was worried you got hurt and that I missed you, and it worked. It really worked! Are you coming home?"

A chill ran up Scooter's spine. Jimmy said he had sent a message to the universe, and Julia had showed up in what Scooter still thought might have been a dream. But there couldn't have been a connection between those things.

"Not yet, but I'll be home soon enough. Don't you worry about a thing. I got everything under control. I have to go now. Be good for your mom. I'll call you again real soon."

"Okay. Bye, and be safe."

Just then, the phone was disconnected, and the call was over. Scooter was sad he couldn't talk longer. He was really happy to hear his brother's voice. Something Jimmy had said made Scooter start thinking about Julia, too. His teacher had told Jimmy to send a message to the universe. Was Julia a classmate of Jimmy's? Did Jimmy know her? She said she was a messenger, relaying messages from kids who missed their family members in the military. Scooter had heard of people throwing thoughts out into the universe. According to them, sometimes the universe made things happen. Still, Scooter thought they were just strange people, the kind who lit scented candles, meditated, and wore crystal necklaces. Maybe they were right about the universe, and their way of life wasn't so far out there. Now he wasn't sure what to think, and he had even more questions about Julia, but still no answers.

Chapter 6
Jimmy's House

"Mom, I have to get to school quickly this morning," Jimmy said. "Could you drive me? I have to talk to Ms Beck before the other kids get there. Please, please, please."

"Why are you in such a hurry?"

"I have to tell her that Scott called me. I have to tell her the messenger angels heard the wish I made. That's why he contacted me."

Jimmy was so happy he talked to Scott that he had to share his news with Ms Beck. He wanted to tell her she was right about how wishes weren't only for birthdays and Christmas. They can be made any time your heart really wants something.

"Angels, what angels?" his mom asked. "Jimmy, honey, what are you talking about?"

"I'll tell you everything if you can drive me."

Jimmy's mom was curious and wanted to know what he was talking about. "I have an appointment with Jenny to get my nails done today. I can drive you to school then go to the salon."

Jimmy couldn't wait to get to school and talk to Ms Beck. He wasn't even worried about the math test that morning. He didn't hate math, but it wasn't his favorite.

Language arts and creative writing were his best subjects. He had a great imagination and loved to write stories. He wrote about planes and helicopters because of the stories Scott told him. One of his favorites he'd written was about a fast food restaurant having a "fly-thru" for helicopters, like a drive-thru for cars. Helicopters could hover long enough to order and pick up their food without having to land.

Jimmy and his mom got into the car, fastened their seat belts, and were ready to go. Their house was the only one in the neighborhood that had a circular driveway. Jimmy liked it because his mom could go halfway around, stop at the front door, and let him out of the car. His mother loved the driveway because she never had to back out into the road. Whenever she'd tried backing out, no matter how careful she was, she'd always hit the curb. For that reason, she hadn't parked her car in the garage for a year.

The best part of having a circular driveway was when he and Scott would come home from going out, and Scott would drive around and around until Jimmy either said stop because he was dizzy or his mother would come outside and tell Scott to "act your age and not your shoe size." Scott was a big kid himself. Even though he was twenty years older than Jimmy, Scott loved playing video games and horsing around. And there was no one better to do that with than his younger brother.

Ralph Waldo Emerson Elementary School was ten minutes away by car, longer by school bus because of all the stops the bus had to make.

"Jimmy, honey," his mom said. "Tell me more about the angels and the wish you made about Scott."

At first, he was hesitant to say anything to his mom. He was worried she might not understand. He also didn't want her to get upset with Ms Beck for talking to him about angels. Certain things teachers weren't supposed to talk about. Like Santa Claus. Whenever one of Jimmy's classmates would ask Ms Beck if Santa was real, she would always say, "It's what you believe in your heart that makes things real, not what I tell you." But he'd told his mom that if she drove him to school, he would tell her. And Scott had always told Jimmy that a real man kept his word and his promises. Even if she was going to get upset, he had to tell her.

"On Monday, when it rained," Jimmy said, "Ms Beck picked my name out of a fishbowl to see who would have lunch with her. I didn't want to have lunch with her, but I didn't want to go into the gym for inside recess, either. Me and Ms Beck started talking about stuff like video games and what games I am good at. Then she asked me if I talked to Scott, and I told her no. I said I was getting really worried that something might have happened to him. That's when she told me that when she is sad or misses someone, she talks to the universe, and the angels hear it and make her wishes come true. When lunchtime was over, and she left the room to get the class from the gym, I went over to the window, opened it, and started talking to the universe and the angels. I felt pretty silly talking out the window, but I really missed Scott, so I thought I would try it, and it worked."

Jimmy's mom wasn't sure what to think. Was it coincidence that Scott called after Jimmy talked to the universe, or had something cosmic truly happened?

"Mom, do you believe that angels or the universe can carry messages like that?"

She had to be very careful how she was going to answer his question. If she said no and told him it was just a coincidence that Scott had called when he did, Jimmy would be heartbroken and probably never believe in anything again. And it wasn't as if she didn't believe in the universe and the mysterious ways it sometimes worked. The truth was that she didn't know enough about it to form an opinion. This wasn't about her; it was about her son and what he believed in.

"Yes, Jimmy, I do believe in angels."

She believed in angels because of her Christian upbringing, but she was thankful they had reached the school. She didn't want to have any more of the conversation at that moment because it would probably be a long one with lots of questions. Jimmy wanted to talk to his teacher before his classmates got there, and she needed to make her hair appointment on time.

Jimmy didn't want to be dropped off at the parent loop in front of the school because kids in the parent loop had to stay in their cars until the bell rang. Kids who walked to school or rode their bicycles could go into the cafeteria and wait for the bell. He told his mom to leave him at the corner, and he would walk the rest of the way. She agreed. She could stay at the corner long enough to see him walk into the building and not have any other parent honk their horn because she wasn't moving fast enough. Once she saw him walk into school, she drove away.

Jimmy rushed into the school with the idea of going straight to his classroom, not the cafeteria. If someone saw him in the hallway, he would say he was going to his class for extra help for the math test. It wasn't the whole truth but he would have to say something to be allowed in the hallway. No way would any teacher or hallway monitor allow him to go to his class before the bell rang. And if there was any extra time before the bell rang, he might talk to Ms Beck about his math test because he did have one or two questions, the first one being would he get full credit if he got the correct answer but didn't show all the work. He hated to show his work, and he thought it was a waste of time, but he knew it would be necessary for those standardized tests he had to take.

Just as Jimmy entered the school, Ms Beck was walking out of the main office. She had a cup of coffee in one hand and a stack of folders in the other.

"Good morning, Jimmy," she said. "You're here bright and early."

"My mother had a hair appointment," he said. "She drove me today. I wanted to talk to you about something. Can I come to class with you?"

"Of course," she said. "Is everything okay? You didn't forget to do your homework, did you?"

"I did my homework," Jimmy said. "I even studied for the math test a little. I have a couple of questions about the test."

He looked around the hallway to see if anyone else was there. What he had to say was really important. He didn't want anyone but Ms Beck to hear it, so he started to whisper. "The universe heard my wish. Scott called me this morning. I still can't believe it. The angels heard me."

They had reached the classroom, and they went inside and shut the door. There was no need to whisper any more because they were the only ones there.

"I told you they would," Ms Beck said. "When you make a wish from your heart, it always comes true. Your wish came true very quickly. I am so happy for you."

She truly was happy for him. Seeing his face light up when he was telling her made her eyes well up with tears of joy.

"Maybe the angels weren't so busy this week, and they needed something to do."

"Perhaps they knew how much you were missing Scott and got right on it. Tell me all about it. Is Scott okay? Is he going to come home soon?"

"Well, the phone rang early this morning," Jimmy said. "Mom and I were sleeping. It rang in the kitchen. We still have a landline. My mom said we need one because our house alarm is hooked up to it. I picked up the phone, said hello, and it was Scott. He said he was doing fine. He misses me, and he doesn't know when he will come home, but everything was under control. I did tell him that you told me to talk to the universe. I don't know if he knew what I was talking about. I didn't have time to explain because he had to go. I might tell him in a letter or wait until he gets home. I'm not sure yet. I'm just happy he called me, and that he is okay."

Even though Ms Beck was Jimmy's teacher, he had begun to think of her as his friend. She understood how it felt having a brother far away and fighting in a war. It's a scary feeling not many people understand.

"Me too, Jimmy," Ms Beck said. "Don't forget to say thank you to the universe and the angels that contacted him. It's really important always to be thankful. Never forget your manners."

"Okay, I won't forget. You sound like my mom. Do all grownups say the same thing about saying please and thank you?"

"Yes, we do, because that's all we heard when we were little, and we couldn't wait until we were old enough to say it to our kids. In my case, my kids are my students."

Teachers are a unique bunch of people. At the beginning of the school year, they have students. As the school year goes by, they build a special connection with everyone. By the end of the school year, those students become their kids.

The morning bell rang. It startled Ms Beck.

"Oh boy, there is the bell." Ms Beck was rushing out of her classroom. "I have to go out and monitor the hallways. You can stay in the classroom unless you need to go to your locker. Thank the universe if you want or wait until later, but I think the sooner, the better."

Jimmy walked over to the window, reached the lever to unlock it, and turned the handle until he'd opened the window enough to make sure the universe was able to hear him. When he had made his wish Monday, it had been raining, and the window wasn't open very much. He didn't know what he was doing and wasn't sure anyone or anything would even take him seriously. At that point, he would have given anything to hear from Scott and to know he was okay.

"Hi again, universe, it's me, Jimmy Andrews from Harrisburg, Pennsylvania. You might remember me; I talked to you on Monday, when it was raining, and I told you that I really missed my older brother, Scott. I have to make this quick because school is about to start, and the kids in my class are about to come into the classroom. I just wanted to say thanks. I know you heard me the other day because Scott called me this morning. Even though he doesn't know when he is coming home, he told me he is okay, and everything is under control. Thanks for hearing me and making my wish come true. I felt silly at the time, but now I know you're real. I gotta go, my class is coming in, bye."

Jimmy closed the window, ran over to his desk, where his backpack was, and took out his homework folder. He headed over to the table where the homework bin was, put his homework there, and returned to his seat.

"Hi Jimmy, I didn't see you on the bus; how did you get here?" asked Charlie.

Jimmy and Charlie had been best friends since Charlie moved to Harrisburg from Boston in the first grade.

"My mom didn't have to go to work today," Jimmy said. "She drove me. I got here early. Ms Beck saw me in the hallway and told me I could come with her to the classroom."

Chapter 7
Ms Beck

Ms Jessica Beck loved her job and her students. She had known she wanted to be a third-grade teacher since she was in third grade herself. She had even told her brother, Matthew, when she was eight-years-old and he picked her up from school one day that she would be a teacher just like Mrs Green. Her third-grade teacher, Mrs Green, was the best teacher she ever had for two reasons: she didn't believe in homework, and she made learning fun. When it was time for creative writing, Mrs Green would give the class a prompt, and they were allowed to write anything they wanted. She would always say, "This is your story, so give it some thought, be creative, and use your imagination." If the story was about flying in a plane, she wanted to know about the clouds the plane was flying through. Were they fluffy white, did they look like marshmallows, or were they dark storm clouds? Ms Beck often found herself telling her students the same thing Mrs Green used to tell her classes: "Make sure I can read your handwriting. I'm a teacher, not a farmer. I can't read chicken scratch."

Ms Beck gave credit to Mrs Green for the way she skillfully used adjectives when writing comments on report cards and notes to parents. Ms Beck wondered if some of the parents really understood that she was criticizing their child in the best possible way. Two years ago, she had a student she liked. He was polite and kind but sometimes a pest. She wanted to get her point across to his parents that their son was as annoying as a mosquito on a summer night when you are trying to sleep, and the only thing you hear is the whining sound in your ear. No matter what you do to swat it away, it always comes back.

She wrote, Dear Mr and Mrs Crenshaw,

David is a unique student, one who has brought my teaching skills to levels I didn't think they could reach. I love music, and some songs remind me of my students. From the first week of school, the song that always comes to mind with David is *Flight of the Bumblebee.*

Their response was, "Thank you very much, Ms Beck. Davey can be a handful at times. To compare him to such a classic song has made us very proud."

Every time she wanted to reach out to his parents to tell them about his behavior, she recalled their response, shook her head, and laughed. They already knew he was a handful, so telling them again about his behavior might have been unnecessary. She never wanted to be rude to any parents or guardians about their child's behavior. Speaking in code allowed Ms Beck to get her point across in a nice way.

As tough as it was, teachers tried not to favor one student over others in their classes. However, they always had one student who seemed to capture their heart. For Ms Beck this year, it was Jimmy. She tried very hard not to let on that he was the one. She didn't want the other kids to tease him about being a teacher's pet. Jimmy was a good student, friendly, conscientious about his work habits, eager to learn, and kind to his classmates. He was an all-around good kid. Jimmy struck a nerve in her, triggered emotions she had not felt in many years and thought she wouldn't feel again. It was about Matthew and all the times he was deployed.

Matt was ten years older than she was. Their parents wanted a big family, but that wasn't meant to be. After many years of trying to have more children, their parents gave up and were happy with Matthew. One day, their mom found out she was going to have another baby. Jessica was a happy surprise and a blessing.

She had always been close to her brother. She loved every minute of spending time with him, and their age difference didn't bother him. Matt was her protector. He put together all the toys she received on Christmas or her birthday. He read her bedtime stories every night. He thought if he had to read *The Three Little Kittens* one more time, he would start to cry like the kittens in the story. He loved Mopsy. That was the nickname he gave Jessica from the time she was born. As a baby, she had a lot of hair, and it flopped all over the place. She looked like a mop top, and the nickname stuck. But only Matt was allowed to call her that. To anyone else, it was either Jess or Jessica.

When Matt was old enough to drive, he would take her with him everywhere. They went to get ice cream, to the Kids' Zone, and even if he just needed to put gas in his car, she was there. He always said before they left the driveway, "Pilot to co-pilot, all buckled up and ready for take-off?" That was his way of making sure her seat belt was buckled, even though he looked in the rearview mirror to double-check that it was. She was old enough to sit in the front seat, but he was hesitant to allow her to sit there. He thought she would be safer sitting in the back, but he knew she would start sitting in the front seat one day. Matt was fascinated with airplanes, helicopters, and the space program. He always told Jessica, "I am going to be the first astronaut to fly to the sun."

"You can't fly to the sun. You're silly," Jessica said. "You will burn up. It's too hot."

"Oh no, I won't," he said. "I will go at night when the sun is sleeping."

Jessica looked at him, shaking her head. "I will never understand boys."

If he didn't make it to the space program, he would be happy flying commercial planes. He knew at a young age he wanted to fly something, anything, when he grew up.

One day when Jessica was twelve-years-old, she and Matt were running errands. She wanted more than anything to sit in the front seat of her brother's Grand Prix but didn't have the guts to ask him. Matt always made her sit in the back. He would never be able to live with himself if anything happened to his little sister and best friend. They both buckled up and headed off.

The first stop was the gas station, then the auto parts store. The calipers always seemed to hang up on their mom's Chevy Beretta, and they needed to be replaced. Matt decided he was going to change the pads and rotors as well. Their mother loved that car, and he wanted to keep up on the maintenance for her.

Once they left the auto parts store, Matt needed to have a conversation with Jessica that wouldn't sit well. He had to tell her he was leaving again. Matt had joined the Air National Guard Reserves when he was eighteen. It was a part of his master plan for his future. Go to a college, major in engineering, and learn how planes, satellites, rockets, and missiles worked. More than anything, he wanted to fly. He thought the best way for that to happen was to join the service, so he had. It had worked out well for him, too. He was able to go to school and still be home. He had been deployed to other states a few times when natural disasters hit. His unit was deployed as added security and to assist first responders from the sky, giving them aerial help rescuing people who had no way of getting to safety from their flooded homes.

Matt finished his errands. Now it was time for a bit of fun and a serious talk with his younger sister and best friend. He had to tell her he was being sent overseas.

"What do you say we go for some ice cream?" asked Matt.

"Really?" Jessica said. "Yes, I want to go for ice cream. Real ice cream, not frozen yogurt or ice cream that is made from tofu. That stuff is horrible."

"You want to go to the place in the mall?" Matt asked. "The one where you can put whatever you want on it?"

"Yes." She rolled her eyes and shook her head. He knew that was her favorite place. "Once again, I will never understand boys."

Top This ice cream shop was always busy. No matter what time it was, people always seemed to want ice cream. What was nice about Top This? Even though it was in the mall, it wasn't in the food court. It was between Best Buy and Macy's towards the back of the building. It had tables and chairs for people who wanted to take a break from shopping, have some ice cream, and not have to deal with the noise of the food court. Matt and Jessica got there at the perfect time. The only other customers, an older couple, were sitting at the table against the back wall. The older lady was eating a sundae. It looked like hot fudge. Her husband had soft serve chocolate ice cream in a waffle cone. Matt knew he wanted the same thing as the older man as soon as he saw it. They walked up to the counter. Matt asked Jessica what she wanted.

"You know what I want. I get the same thing every time." Jessica rolled her eyes again.

The girl behind the counter laughed. "I am the youngest of six. I did the same thing to my older brother. Now, what can I get you?"

Matt shook his head. "I feel for your brother. I will have chocolate in a waffle cone, please. My snarky sister will have vanilla ice cream with rainbow sprinkles and a cherry on top in a sugar cone."

He paid for the ice cream and made his way over to the table, where Jessica was already sitting. He handed over her cone and sat down. She was fighting with the sprinkles, trying to eat them before the ice cream melted and it all ended up being sprinkle soup. He was trying to capture this moment of his little sister's innocence because what he was about to tell her wasn't going to be easy.

"Jess," he said. "There is something I have to say. You might not like it."

"Oh no, don't say it. There is another hurricane somewhere, and you have to leave."

"Not exactly. I do have to go and help. But I am going to Bosnia."

Jessica looked at him as if he had grown a second nose. He did say she wouldn't like it. He was wrong. She hated it. To hold back from crying, she started asking him every question she thought of.

"Where are you going? I never heard of that place. That's not a state. What are you going to be doing?"

"No, it's not a state, Jess. It's a different country."

"A different country? How long will you be gone? I don't want you to go. Quit the Army. Tell them you changed your mind."

The tears started to flow. Matt had known it wasn't going to go over well, but he didn't think she would have a complete meltdown.

Jessica felt someone's hand on her shoulder. She looked up, and it was the girl from behind the counter. Her name tag said, Patti.

"Is everything okay?" Patti asked.

"No, everything is wrong, bad, and stupid," Jessica cried.

"Jess, I promise you everything is going to be okay." Matt tried to calm her down.

"Is there anything I can do to help?" Patti said.

"I'm in the Army, and my unit is being deployed. We are leaving on Saturday."

"SATURDAY," Jessica screamed. She put her cone down, folded her arms, and put her head on the table, staring at her feet. No way was she going to look at her older brother, no matter what he was saying.

"Mops, you know I have a job to do. I left before, and I came back. This time I will be away a little longer, but I will be back."

Patti looked at Matt. "Can I cut in for a second? It seems your sister and I have more in common than just being the youngest."

"Absolutely," Matt said. "I can use all the help you can give me."

"Honey," Patti said to Jessica. "Can you look at me for just a second?"

Jessica wasn't looking up. She didn't care who was talking or what they had to say.

Matt was not going to allow his younger sister to be rude or disrespectful to Patti when she was only trying to help.

"Jessica, I know you are mad at me, and that's fine. But you will not be rude to Patti. Pick your head up and listen."

Jessica picked up her head slowly.

"You know, I am the youngest of six kids. I understand how you feel. My older brother is a soldier too. He is in the Marines. When he is away, I miss him a lot. He is away now. He is in Japan, and he had to go to some scary places. I was really worried I would never see him again. When he came home he told me even he was afraid," Patti said. "Sometimes, he couldn't contact or write to us. But he and I have a special way of talking to each other. Maybe it will work for you and your brother. If you want to know about it, I can tell you."

Jessica was all ears. "Yes, please, I want to know."

"Okay, but it will be our secret. Younger sister to younger sister."

Patti looked at Matt as if to say, can you please leave us alone for a minute? Matt knew when to take a hint. He excused himself and walked over to the bulletin board to read about the latest news in ice cream.

"When John, that's my brother, was away, especially in dangerous places," Patti told Jessica, "I was always scared something bad would happen to him. I would go outside, find a quiet place. Finally I sent a message to him from my heart through the universe.

"I said, 'Hi universe, It's Patti Shea. My brother John Shea is a Marine. He is far away, and I miss him. Can you please tell him I love him and miss him and want him to write to me as soon as possible? Thank you.' You always have to make sure you thank the universe. It's really important. When you send messages from your heart into the universe, angels hear them. They deliver the messages to the person you are missing most. In my case, it was always my brother. I promise you if you do the same thing when your brother is away, he will get the message and contact you as soon as he can, just the way John did."

"Is that a real story?" Jessica asked. Or was it just a story to make her feel better because Matt was leaving?

"It's a real story," Patti said. "You can come back now," she said to Matt.

"Thank you for coming to my rescue," Matt said.

"You're welcome."

It was time for Matt and Jessica to leave the ice cream shop and head home. Jessica got up from her chair and hugged Patti.

"Thank you; I feel better," Jessica said. "I hope your brother comes home soon."

"You're very welcome, sweetheart," Patti said. "Me too."

Patti hugged Matt as well. "Be safe, and come and see me when you get back."

"Count on it," Matt said.

As they left the ice cream shop, Matt asked Jessica if she wanted to sit in the front seat. She looked at him with the biggest, brightest smile. Even though he thought she would still be safer in the back, she was getting older, and he needed to start treating her appropriately.

"How did you know I wanted to sit in the front?"

"When I was twelve, I did sit in the front. Now, you can too."

The day Matt was leaving came, and it was the most horrible day of the year for Jessica. She decided that from now on, until Matt came home, Saturday was going to be the worst day of the week for her. It was the day Matt was leaving for Bosnia, so it must be the worst day ever. Matt was already at the base, making sure he had everything he needed.

As his parents and Jessica drove through the Stratton Air National Guard Base gates, Jessica saw the bus. That was when she finally knew it wasn't a rumor, and her big brother was going away. It's always just a rumor until you see the white bus at the base. Matt's parents were waiting for him by a fence, with all the other fathers and mothers saying goodbye to their sons or daughters. He hugged his dad, then his mom. They told him they loved him and were proud of him. He turned to Jessica. He picked her up and hugged her.

"I'll write to you as soon as I can."

"I'll write back. I promise."

Matt got onto the bus and waved goodbye.

Chapter 8
Ms Beck's Classroom

The school year was progressing just as Ms Beck had hoped it would. The conscientious students were working as hard as ever. Their homework was always done, classwork always completed. The students who did anything but classwork and never did their homework continued on their path of doing nothing with complete support from their parents. Ms Beck was amazed at how some parents justified their children not doing homework. One letter had always stood out in her memory.

Dear Ms Beck,

Please excuse Eli for not doing his homework last night. Our neighbor's 96-year-old aunt died in Michigan, and we had to go over to her house to console her. He is a sensitive child and felt so bad for our neighbor he couldn't do his homework.

Thank you,
Mr and Mrs Little

After she read the note, she couldn't justify excusing him again. His parents always had an explanation as to why Eli couldn't do his homework. It was happening weekly, and she needed to put a stop to it. She gave him a zero but offered him a chance to make it up with a half credit if he did it that night, along with the current homework assignment. His parents may not have liked Eli receiving a zero or half credit, but Ms Beck needed for them to understand that the little homework she did assign needed to be completed.

She didn't want to be a strict or mean teacher. She understood that in life, things we don't have any control of happen. However, she also wanted her students to understand they had responsibilities, and homework was one of them, especially with the horrible week of standardized testing that was fast approaching.

When she was a kid, Ms Beck hated taking the state-mandated tests. As a teacher, she hated administering them. She understood why they were given. It was the state's way of seeing if students were learning to their grade level. But it was all nonsense as far as she was concerned. She would teach the way she wanted to teach in her classroom and make sure her students understood the lessons. That's what was important to her.

But she wasn't going to worry about that right now. It was one fifteen, time for social studies.

"Boys and girls," Ms Beck said, "whatever vocabulary you didn't finish, take it home and finish it there."

As her students put all their books away, she started thinking about Matt and the project she was going to have her students do this year. The social studies curriculum in third grade was American history and geography. The kids had to learn the states, their capitals, and their locations on the map. They had to learn where the oceans were located and how to read the directions on a compass rose. But since this year's curriculum in social studies was American history, Ms Beck had thought of doing something completely different with her students. Rather than having the kids write book reports about the presidents or other famous people in American history, she had come up with the idea to contact the local Veterans of Foreign War hall to see if some of the veterans would like to come and discuss their military service with her class. They would have a question-and-answer session. The students could ask the veterans questions about their roles and responsibilities as soldiers, if they were deployed overseas and where they went. The more she thought about her idea, the more she liked it. She would ask her brother if he would come to talk to her class about his time in the military. He wasn't on the front lines any more. Now he had a desk job in Washington, D.C.

Jessica loved that Matt worked in Washington and loved being able to visit him any time she wanted. She didn't have to worry about him getting hurt or when he was going to come home. She and her brother were still as close as ever, and Matt's wife, Patti, had been her best friend from the day they met in Top This, Patti's older brother's ice cream shop in the mall, when Jessica was twelve. Jessica took credit for bringing Matt and Patti together. She always said that if she hadn't had a tantrum in the ice cream shop, Patti would have never come over to their table to try and calm her down, and Matt would have never had a conversation with Patti.

She was waiting for her students to get themselves organized and sit in their seats, but it could take them a while to quieten down, especially if the girls started talking. Ms Beck had to start the social studies lesson because explaining it to them could take the rest of the afternoon.

"Boys and girls," she said, "settle down and take out your history books."

"Ms Beck," Emma called out, "why do we have to learn all this stuff?"

"Please remember to raise your hand if you have a question."

Ms Beck needed to remind the kids almost every day to raise their hands when they wanted to ask her something. If they didn't raise their hands, she would not acknowledge their questions. Emma just called out her question, and Ms Beck ignored her.

Emma looked at Ms Beck and wanted so badly to roll her eyes at her as if to say, I just asked you a question, but you wouldn't answer it because I didn't raise my hand. She had rolled her eyes at Ms Beck once earlier in the school year, and Ms Beck had taken away her recess for a whole week. Emma must have remembered her punishment, because she raised her hand.

"Yes, Emma," Ms Beck said. "You have a question?"

"Why do we have to learn all this stuff?" Emma asked. "Whenever my parents take us anywhere, they put the address in the GPS."

Emma was a nice girl, and Ms Beck enjoyed having her in her class, but she was a bit of a know-it-all.

"Well," Ms Beck said, "suppose one day your GPS isn't working properly, or you can't use the map app on your phone because the battery is low and you forgot the charger. You have to know which direction you are traveling in to get to where you need to be. A good old-fashioned paper map or an atlas is always good to have in your car."

Emma was right. Most parents now used a GPS when they were driving someplace they had never been before. However, when Jessica was a little girl, her parents always had an atlas in the car. They used it mostly to plan their trip when they were going on vacation.

Some of the kids were confused. A few asked the person next to them, "What's an atlas?" No one had an answer.

"Okay, class." Ms Beck started the lesson. "We already learned where the states are and their capitals. But for some reason, when we learned about how to read a compass, I should have shown you what an atlas was. It's not a part of this new lesson, but we can take a few minutes and talk about an atlas. Raise your hand if you think you know what it is."

No one knew, or perhaps they were afraid of giving the wrong answer and being laughed at by the other kids.

"So," Ms Beck said. "An atlas is a book of maps with all the roads in the United States in it. It has highways, service roads, country roads. It also has many other things like national forests, mountains, states, their capitals, and boundary lines. It has all sorts of information. I have one in my car. I will bring it tomorrow so you can take a look at it."

That seemed to curb their curiosity for the time being. The kids might have a few questions tomorrow. Once they were able to look through it, she would be happy to answer them.

"Our next lesson is about how we became the great country we are and what it took to get us there," she said. "But instead of giving you a book report and a project to do, we are going to do something different."

Before she could go on, right on schedule, Eli interrupted her. He was her sensitive student, and at times, her rude student, and he loved to voice his opinion about everything.

"I bet it's going to be something boring," Eli shouted. "Like dressing up as our favorite person from history when we don't even know anyone from then because they are all dead."

"Eli," Ms Beck said. "You lose ten minutes of recess tomorrow."

"What? Why?" Eli said.

"For being rude and disrespectful."

It was one thing for a student not to raise their hand. It was another thing to be rude. She knew she would get an email or note from Eli's parents telling her how sorry Eli was for being rude. His parents would probably ask her to allow him to have recess because recess was important to a child's well-being.

Not having a rude student was important to her well-being and how she ran her classroom. Maybe she would send his parents an email first. She could be proactive instead of waiting for the inevitable email from them.

"No, it's not going to be boring at all. We will go to the library tomorrow, and you can do research on any war from the Korean War up to Desert Storm 2. Then I want you to think of questions you might want to ask a soldier. I am making a plan to contact the local VFW hall. That stands for Veterans of Foreign Wars. I will ask if any soldier would like to come and speak to us and answer your questions. That will be in two weeks, on Friday the eighteenth. So, now that you know your project, take out your social studies book and turn to page two hundred and fifty one."

As the afternoon went on, Jimmy became withdrawn and quiet. He did his work, but all this talk about veterans was probably bothering him. Even though he had gotten to talk to Scott briefly the other day, Jimmy still wasn't himself.

***

It was three p.m., time for dismissal. Jimmy got on the bus and sat in the first seat behind the driver. He wanted to be alone, and sitting behind the driver would almost guarantee that. No one ever wanted to sit directly behind the driver. The back of the bus was always more fun and much louder. Jimmy stared out the window, thinking about Scott and wishing he would come home. The only bright spot about the day was that Scott had promised to get in touch with him when he was no longer under a no-communication order. Like he did every day, Jimmy hoped today might be the day that Scott could call him.

The bus dropped him off on his corner, and he walked the rest of the way home. He was eight-years- old, and that was too old to have his mother waiting to meet him. She had reluctantly agreed to let him walk by himself. She wanted Jimmy to gain his sense of independence but still worried about his safety. However, because they only lived four houses from the bus stop, she could wait for him outside and she could see him walk home without embarrassing him.

"Hi, honey." She stopped weeding the rock garden when she saw Jimmy coming up the driveway. "How was your day?"

"Okay, I guess. You think Scott will call today?"

"I don't know, sweetheart. I'm sure he will call you as soon as he can. I made you a snack. It's on the counter. I'll be in as soon as I put the garden tools away."

"Okay, Mom. It's just that we have a social studies project, and I thought it would be great if Scott could be there."

"You know, honey," she said, "if he could be there, he would be."

By the look on his face and the way Jimmy walked into the house, it was going to be a long night. If Scott did call, Jimmy would be fine, and it would maybe even put a smile on his face.

At four thirty, Jimmy was doing his homework at the kitchen table. His mother had come inside, made herself a cup of coffee, sat down at her computer in the hallway, and was browsing the internet. Her computer started beeping, and she thought she had done something wrong, but it was the sound an incoming call makes from Skype. Jimmy heard it as well.

"That's Scott, Mom," Jimmy said. "Hit the green answer button."

He had to answer Scott's call quickly or he might lose the signal. The signal strength can be so unpredictable, and Jimmy didn't want to take a chance of anything going wrong. His mom knew if Jimmy had a chance to speak to Scott, it would cheer him up. She hit the answer button. There was Scott.

"Hi, Scott," Jimmy's mom, Barbara, said. "How are you?"

"Hey, Barbie Doll," Scott said. "I'm doing as well as can be expected."

Scott always called Barbara "Barbie Doll." It was his nickname for her, a play on her name and the fact she had blonde hair. Technically, she was his stepmother. Within six months of Scott's parents getting divorced, Barbara had married his father. Over the years, they had developed a good friendship. After Jimmy was born, they grew into a family.

"I'm sure you are. Please be careful," she said. "Here's Jimmy. I'll leave you boys alone to talk."

"Hi, Scott," Jimmy said. "How are you?"

"Hey, buddy," Scott said. "I'm doing okay. I'm doing a lot of flying at night. The no-communication order was just lifted, so I thought I would give you a call."

"I hope it lasts so we can talk more," Jimmy said. "Do you get to wear the night vision glasses?"

"I sure do. Are you behaving for your mom? Helping her out if she needs help?"

"Sometimes," Jimmy said. "Do you think you will be coming home in two weeks?"

"I don't think so," Scott said. "Hopefully, it will be soon, no worries."

"Next Friday in school, we are having soldiers come and talk to us from the VF-something or other. I can't remember what Ms Beck said. I was hoping you would be there."

"I would if I could. You know that. But there is just no way. We were just told we will be here until at least Thanksgiving."

Jimmy's face fell. He couldn't believe Scott was going to be away until Thanksgiving.

"Thanksgiving? That's in November. It's June, so that's still a long time away. You said you would be home for the Fourth of July," Jimmy said. "We were going to go to Daytona to see the race this year, remember?"

Scott felt horrible, and seeing the look of disappointment on Jimmy's face, he felt as if he had been punched in the gut. He hated to disappoint his little brother. But there was nothing he could do. "I'm sorry, buddy."

"It's okay. I understand. It's just that Ms Beck's brother will be there. I wanted you to be there too. But I know orders are orders."

Before Scott could answer, he lost his signal. The last thing he saw was the disappointment on Jimmy's face. Usually, Scott loved his job, but he wasn't sure if he hated his job, himself, or both after seeing Jimmy's face.

Chapter 9
Watchtower Harbor

June in Watchtower Harbor was always full of activity. School was finishing up for the year. Signs congratulating Watchtower High seniors were popping up along Route Eighteen, the main road in and out of town. Ferry boats started coming into the harbor after the winter break, bringing happy tourists eager to spend their money on useless keepsakes, overpriced dinners, and sitting in the world's worst traffic jams just to get to the beach to fight with other tourists over a parking spot. Then they walked three miles on burning sand to find the perfect place to plant their beach chairs, umbrellas, and coolers full of all sorts of drinks that resembled the rainbow, and they all tasted like the plastic containers they came in. Other than that, the town was truly a throwback to a simpler time, when a kid's toughest choices were between vanilla or chocolate ice cream in a waffle or a sugar cone, with rainbow or chocolate sprinkles.

Both Julia and Sophie were excited not only because school was ending but also to see all the tourists filling up the beaches. For them, it meant meeting new kids from other places and becoming friends with them for however long their vacation was. Most of the time, it was one week, but sometimes it was two weeks. The girls were always saddened when their new friends left. They wished their new friends could spend the whole summer and not go back home until school started in September.

One of the reasons the girls loved meeting new people from distant places was because they would always go home and locate where the kids were from on the maps on their wall.

The past couple of days, Annalise, the girls' mother, had noticed that Julia wasn't quite herself. At first, she thought it was her allergies acting up because that time of year, everything was blooming. The lilac trees were in full bloom. Their bunches of lavender flowers looked beautiful against dark green heart-shaped leaves. When the wind was blowing off the water, you could smell the lilacs throughout the house. The rosebushes all had buds on them. They would probably bloom within the week. Once again, the streets in town were lined with bright red geraniums hanging from the black wrought-iron lamp posts, making the sidewalk look like Buckingham Palace guards were protected it. Apart from the traffic, this was a fun time of year for Watchtower Harbor.

Annalise wondered if Julia's allergies were bothering her or something else. If it was her allergies, they could shut the windows in the family room to watch TV until the wind died down. She decided to ask her.

"Julia," Annalise said. "Are you feeling okay, honey?"

"I feel fine," Julia answered. "Why?"

"You don't look fine," her mom said. "You look as if something is bothering you."

"I do feel a little strange," Julia said. "Kinda like something is going to happen, but I don't know what."

"Does it feel like a wish?" her mom asked.

Since the girls were able to hear wishes from children who had family members who were deployed, Annalise always checked to see if it was a desire they were picking up on, or if the girls were really not feeling well.

"I don't know," Julia said. "It might be. I'm not sure. Maybe I'll feel better if I go in the backyard and water the flowers."

"Okay," her mom said. "Sounds like a good idea. Just be careful you don't trip on the hose. In the meantime, I will go and check on your sister. Maybe she wants to water the flower beds in the front."

On her way inside Annalise stopped and picked up the can to water the impatiens that were hanging in baskets on the shepherd's hook. They were too high for Julia to reach, and Annalise didn't want her daughter to use the hose to water them.

The girls' gift had come from her. When she was a little girl, she had also been able to hear wishes from other children and grant them. She never told anyone except her mom. She was afraid that if she told her friends or her sister, they would think she was weird and wouldn't want to play with her. She never wanted her girls to feel different, so she kept the fact she could also hear wishes when she was a little girl to herself. As they got older, she would tell them and hope they would find husbands as understanding as Sean was.

When she'd told Sean about her gift, she had been terrified of what his reaction would be. Her hands had been trembling, her voice had cracked, and she had almost started to cry. It took her a couple of minutes and a few deep breaths before she was able to start talking.

"I hear people talking to me," she said, "people that I don't know and have never met speak to me."

"Go on." Sean said. He was trying to understand what she was saying without changing his facial expression. He didn't want her to think he was making fun of her or that he thought she was crazy.

"It started after my mother passed away. I would talk to her because I missed her. I would talk to her about how my day was or if someone was bothering me. If there was a boy in my class I thought was cute, I would tell her. She would answer me as if she was still alive and sitting right next to me. She would come to me in my dreams, which I thought was normal. But she would also come to me whenever I was alone."

"What's wrong with that?" Sean asked. "You were a little girl that just lost her mother. You missed her."

So far, he didn't think anything was that unusual about her. She was a little girl who wished her mom was still alive and talking to her as if she still was.

"There's more." She took a deep breath. "This is where things get very strange, and I didn't know what to do."

"Okay. I'm still here, and I'm listening," he said.

"One day," she said, "I was probably eleven-years-old. I heard a different voice. I was used to hearing only my mother's voice. I looked around. I thought she was standing behind me. She wasn't. It was a little girl's voice. She was talking out loud, I guess, to the sky. I can remember everything she said.

"She said, 'Dear universe, my name is Jessica. I am ten-years-old, and I am really sad. I miss my older brother, Matt. He is in the Army and really far away. He hasn't written to me in a long time and I'm really scared something has happened to him. Could you send him a message and tell him to write to me as soon as he can?'"

"Wow," Sean said. "That's pretty powerful coming from a ten-year-old."

He wanted to be understanding and supportive and not have any kind of reaction, good or bad. He loved Annalise and didn't want her to be scared of telling him anything, not now or in the future.

"I knew I had to help her. But I didn't know what to do. I was eleven-years-old. I couldn't tell anyone I heard voices."

"No, I guess you couldn't."

"That night, when I went to bed, I couldn't sleep. I had to help Jessica. I fell asleep thinking about what I could do. Here is the scary part. I told myself it was a dream, but I know it wasn't. Somehow while I was asleep, I actually went to where Matt was and talked to him. He was in Bosnia. I told him not to be afraid of me. I said I had a message from Jessica. I asked him to write or call her if he could, because she was sad and missed him. She thought something bad might have happened to him."

"Telepathy?" Sean asked. "I've heard of that."

He had heard of people being telepathic, but he'd thought people had to work at it, not that it came naturally. He didn't think it could happen at such a young age, either, but then again he didn't know much about it.

"Two days later," she said, "I heard Jessica's voice again. She was thanking the universe. Her brother was able to call her, and he was fine."

"Is that it?" Sean breathed a sigh of relief. "That's what you were afraid to tell me? I don't see that as such a big deal."

"What do you mean?" Annalise said. "Aren't you freaked out, even a little bit? Suppose we do get married and have children, and one of them can hear voices."

"You will be a great mother, and I will be a great dad," he said. "We will help them understand the special gift they have and how to deal with it together."

She'd been daydreaming, and had never watered the impatiens. They would have to wait. She wanted to find Sophie and ask her if she wanted to water the flowers. She went into the girl's bedroom where Sophie was playing house with her dolly. It was nap time for dolly. Sophie laid her dolly in the bassinet that she and her sister had slept in when they were babies. She covered her with the pink-and-purple blanket that had come with the doll when her father gave it as a present to Sophie last year after one of his missions.

"Mom," said Sophie, "when is Daddy coming home?"

"One day very soon, sweetheart."

Annalise was never sure when her husband would be home. She always responded with the same generic answer: one day, very soon. Being the wife of a SEAL wasn't easy. She worried constantly, and never knowing his whereabouts, whether he was safe, or when he was coming home, caused her to have many sleepless nights.

***

Julia had been hoping if she watered the garden, her thoughts would clear up, and she might understand why she was feeling strange. When a wish from a child was coming, she knew what to expect and how to feel. Now, her feelings were entirely different but at the same time familiar. She was restless and jumpy. It was like someone needed her, someone she had helped before, but she couldn't figure out who it was or what they needed. Whatever, it was exhausting. She was so tired. She decided to stop watering the vegetable garden and sit on the lounge chair underneath the oak tree. It was her favorite tree. When her father was home from a mission, she would pack a picnic lunch that consisted of roast beef sandwiches, her father's favorite, pickles, and fruit punch. The tree stood eighty feet tall with over a million leaves on it. At least, that's what her father used to say about the leaves because he was the one stuck raking them every year.

 She must have fallen asleep because the next thing she felt was Sophie shaking her arm, telling her to wake up. Julia was disoriented, and it took her a second to figure out where she was. She was outside under the oak tree. She wanted to be alone for a bit longer to wake up and remember why she was outside to begin with. The last thing she needed was her little sister pestering her.

"Go inside," Julia said. "I think I hear your dolly crying."

"She isn't crying," Sophie answered. "Mommy is with her."

"Go inside anyway, and leave me alone."

"I'm going, and I am telling Mommy you went to sleep and the tomatoes won't grow, and she won't have anything for her salad for the whole summer, and you will be in big trouble."

"If you don't go inside and leave me alone, I will turn the water back on and water you instead of the tomatoes."

As aggravated as Julia was by being woken up and pestered by her sister, she made herself laugh by saying that to her.

"Now I'm really telling." Sophie ran away, yelling, "Mommy, Julia said she was going to water me instead of the tomatoes."

Julia sat there for a few more minutes, trying to figure out if a dream or a wish had come to her while she was sleeping, or both. Either way, she realized whose feelings she had been picking upon. They were Scott's. This was different. Up until this point, she had only heard wishes from children, never from grownups. She ran inside the house to tell her mother what her dream, wish, or feeling was about. She wasn't sure what it was, but she was scared because nothing like this had ever happened.

"Mommy," Julia yelled from the yard.

"I'm in the living room, honey."

Annalise was checking her emails and playing solitaire online. Solitaire was her escape and solace when missing her husband was too much for her.

"Mommy, Scott needs my help. You remember Scott. He is the soldier I went to see in Afghanistan. His brother was Jimmy. Remember?"

"Of course, I remember."

"Why am I getting wishes from grownups, Mom?" Julia asked. "It's always been just from kids."

Annalise didn't have an answer for that. When she was little, the only wishes she had ever gotten were from children. She had to think fast and come up with an answer.

"Well, hmm," she said. "Maybe it's because you already went to Scott and talked to him, and you picked up on his feelings about missing his brother. I bet he wants to come home."

"Should I be scared?"

"Oh no, sweetheart, not at all. A soldier would never hurt you. Their job is to protect us and keep us safe."

Annalise was happy with that answer, considering she didn't have more than half a second to think of it.

"I know, Mommy," Julia said. "Daddy tells me the same thing. When is he coming home?"

"One day, very soon."

Annalise once again went to her generic answer. But it worked, and when she said it, the girls didn't keep asking her over and over again about their dad and when he was coming back. Now, the best thing to do was change the subject and ask Julia about her dream.

"Tell me about your dream," she said. "What happened with Scott?"

"I think he wants to come home because his brother is having a special day for soldiers in school, and he wanted to be there. He can't get back, and he was sad about it."

"I'm sure he wants to come home," her mom said, "just like Daddy wants to always be home with us. But he has a job to do, and so does Scott."

"I know, Mommy. But he was so lovely when I went to him. I want to help him. In my dream, he was talking to another man. He called him Mike. I think Mike is the one in charge, like Daddy. He looked much older than Daddy. He had gray hair and everything."

"He might be," Annalise said. "Daddy doesn't have any gray hair yet."

Julia was looking at her mother's computer screen, wondering why her mother played this game. Seven rows of black and red cards, it didn't look like a lot of fun to her. She thought grownups did a lot of strange things. That was one of them. I'm not going to do strange things when I grow up, Julia thought.

"I'm going to help Scott, Mommy. Tonight."

She went to the wall maps to remind herself exactly where Afghanistan was. She found it and knew what she needed to do to help get Scott home.

***

Kandahar, Afghanistan
Mike's Office

The flight crew had just left another meeting with Mike. It seemed these meetings were getting longer and more frequent. Everyone hated them, but they had to be done. The meetings would have been even worse if someone other than Mike were commander. Everyone who worked with Mike loved him. He led from the front. He would never ask his men to do anything he wouldn't do first. Some of the people in Washington, especially the Pentagon, didn't like Mike very much. They felt he acted too much like "one of the boys" rather than a high-ranking officer. They had to respect his rank but nothing more after that.

After reading his reports about the last mission, the powers that be in Washington thought more things should be done in the way of scouting and trying to find out what was being stored in the warehouse. Mike wished he could tell the brass in Washington that they could come fly the scouting missions themselves, and he could go fishing! However, if he ever said that to them, it would be followed by a court-martial and perhaps prison time. So, best keep his thoughts to himself and go fishing when he got home.

Mike had had enough for the day. It was a thousand degrees outside. The meetings were over. It was a good time to lie down for a while and forget what was going on around him. He fell asleep as soon as his head hit his pillow. He woke up about an hour later because he heard a noise in his tent. Someone was in there with him, which wasn't all that unusual. Sometimes someone needed something and had to wake him up. This time was different. He was right about the presence. It wasn't a soldier. It was a little girl. He wasn't completely awake, not yet. He rubbed his eyes, and she was still there. He wasn't sure what to think or what to do. Why would a little girl be in his tent? When she started to talk, she knew his name.

"Hi Mike, my name is Julia, and my mother told me to tell you not to be afraid of me. People think they see a ghost, but I'm not a ghost. I'm a special little girl, one who is just a little different than other kids my age. I'm a messenger. I bring messages to soldiers that are away from kids in their families that really miss them. I don't have a message from a child this time, but Scott's brother, Jimmy, has a special day coming up at school and really wants Scott to be there. I know you are in charge, and you can send people home when it's an emergency. My daddy had to do that once, for one of his soldiers, so you can too."

Still groggy, Mike sat up in his bunk, trying to make sense of what was happening. He started talking to her, and she responded. He had to figure out what was going on.

"Your daddy is a soldier?" Mike asked.

"Yes," she said. "He is the best soldier in the world."

Mike smiled because both of his kids had said the same thing about him.

"I'm sure he is."

"Can you send Scott home? Jimmy needs him. It's an emergency."

"Is he sick or hurt?"

Mike was afraid that something bad had happened to Jimmy. He knew how close Scott was to his brother. Mike thought the world of Jimmy as well. If something had happened to him, how was he going to tell Scott?

"No," Julia said. "He has a special day at school, and Jimmy wants Scott to be there."

"Julia, it's not that easy," Mike said. "I can't just send Scott home. It wouldn't be fair to the other soldiers. If I send him home, everyone will have an emergency and want to go home. We have a job to do, and we can't go home until it's done."

If it were up to Mike, he would send his men home every weekend. But the best he could do was make sure the satellite signal was strong enough that they could talk to their families more than once a week.

"My daddy always said, 'you won't know unless you try. You have to do the impossible first'."

"Is your daddy in the Army?"

"No, he is a SEAL."

"That figures," Mike said. "Those guys are crazy, to begin with."

Too late, Mike realized what he'd said about this beautiful little girl's father. Julia had a wounded look in her eyes.

"I'm sorry, Julia. That came out wrong. I wasn't calling your father crazy. Some of the things SEALs do to keep the world safe are crazy."

"You don't have to apologize," she said. "My daddy always said the Army gets the easy work."

Mike deserved that. For a girl with an angelic face, she cut right to the quick.

"Will you help Scott go home?" Julia asked again.

"I think I can get him home for a couple of days."

Now he had to think about how he was going to pull this off. He might be able to pull a few strings, call in a couple of favors. But it would be easier to hide a helicopter behind a palm tree than to think of a good reason to get Scott home. No pressure at all.

Julia smiled and clapped her hands with excitement and walked out the door. It Mike ever mentioned this to anyone, they would give him a Section 8 discharge, and he would never get his pension. His dream of hanging up a sign that said GONE FISHING would be over. It would be replaced with a sign that said GONE CRAZY.

Chapter 10
Harrisburg, Pennsylvania

Ms Beck was going to lose her mind. The end of the school year was always a stressful time. Principal, Elaine Stone told her she had to move her classroom from one side of the school to the other to make room for the new S.T.E. M. (science, technology, engineering, and math) class. Ralph Waldo Emerson Elementary School had won a ten thousand dollar grant from the Department of Education to integrate S.T.E.M. into the school's curriculum. It would be on a trial basis to see if it helped students learn and become more interested in math and science with a more hands-on approach. Ms Beck didn't mind moving her classroom. Her new classroom would be bigger and brighter. It was on the east side of the building and would get more of the morning sun than the classroom she had now. She was also thrilled because she had applied for the grant and beat three other schools in the district.

Also on Ms Beck's mind was her question-and-answer project with the veterans. That day was approaching faster than she thought. She had a first-rate lineup of veterans. They had been kind enough to volunteer their time to come to her class, talk to the kids, and answer their questions. She had an even mix of men and women who had served abroad in conflicts ranging from the Korean War to Afghanistan.

When her students were researching the wars in the school library, Billy was online looking for information about the Korean War. His grandfather had been in the Army in the 1950s and was sent to Korea. Billy was getting more and more upset. Every time he searched for "Korean War" on the internet, "Korean Conflict" popped up. He shouted at the computer, "It wasn't a conflict. It was a war. My grandpa said so."

Trying to understand war at any age was difficult enough, but when a war was never formally declared by the government, things get even more complicated.

Ms Beck thought it would be good to talk to Billy and try to calm him down.

"Billy," Ms Beck said. "Can you come here, please?"

Before she could finish her sentence, he interrupted her.

"I didn't do anything," Billy said. "I can't be in trouble. I didn't do anything."

He was so used to getting into trouble either at home or in school that he started to defend himself before he even knew why his name was being called.

"Everything is fine," she said. "I just want to talk to you."

He went the long way around every table and chair in the library, hoping to delay the talk with Ms Beck.

"Let's sit over here," she said, "away from the rest of the class."

He sat in the chair opposite hers. He was close enough to hear but far enough away so that if the other kids saw him, they wouldn't think he was getting in trouble. Everyone in the class knew that if Ms Beck wanted you to sit close to her or took you into the hallway, you were in a bad situation.

"Billy," she said. "I know how you feel about your grandfather. It's the same way I feel about my brother, very proud."

"Your brother was in the Korean War, too?" he said with disbelief. If her brother was an old man, how old was she?

"No, silly." She laughed. "That would make my brother older than my father."

They both started to laugh.

"What I wanted to say," she continued, "is that the words they use to describe the Korean War are words only the government cares about. The soldiers that were sent there did the job they were asked to do. They did it the best way they knew how and did a good job. So, don't pay too much attention to those words. It was a war. I know you are proud your grandpa was a part of that, and you should be. Now get back to your research and make me proud. If you need help, raise your hand. I'll come right over. No more shouting, okay?"

"Okay." Billy nodded. "I can't wait to call my grandpa tonight and tell him I'm researching the Korean War."

Ms Beck gave him a big smile as he went back to the computer. Billy was a bit all over the place. That's why he was recommended for an IEP from other teachers. She never could understand why other teachers had such a difficult time with him. He wasn't a cookie-cutter type of student, but she liked that about him. He challenged her, making her think more as a teacher. What were his educational needs? How did she keep a bright student engaged without boring him? She asked herself those questions regularly, not just about Billy but many of her students.

***

Kandahar, Afghanistan

Lt. Colonel Michael Cullen of Central Command was still trying to wrap his head around the dream he'd had, or was it a vision? Who was this little girl, and why had she come to him? She'd said her name was Julia, explained who she was and why she was there. She looked real, and the conversation had felt very real. Still, it didn't make any sense. Why had she asked for Scott to go home? Every kid has events at school that parents, or in this case siblings, miss. Perhaps it was more than just an event at school, and maybe something had happened to Jimmy, even though she'd said that wasn't it. A million thoughts went through Mike's head. June 18 was a week away, and he had to come up with a good reason to send Scott home without getting himself or Scott into trouble. How could Mike make an exception for Scott when all the other men and women under his command also wanted to go home and see their families? Mike didn't want to show Scott any special treatment. As his commander, Mike couldn't and wouldn't do that. Scott would hate getting special treatment and wouldn't allow Mike to do it, either. Well, maybe he could send Scott to Washington to meet with the commander of Central Command to discuss face to face what they would like to do with the warehouses Scott and his team had kept a close eye on over the past couple of months.

The more Mike thought about it, the more he liked this idea. Scott or someone else might see through Mike's story and call him out for lying. But he could justify sending Scott to Washington because of all the scouting missions Scott and his team had done. Since Harrisburg was only a two-hour drive depending on traffic, why not arrange for the meeting and get Scott home, and hopefully he could see Jimmy and spend the day at school with him?

"Badger, get Washington on the phone," Mike shouted.

Badger was the nickname Mike had given his company clerk because he was constantly pestering Mike about things he needed to do or sign. Mike liked Badger. He was a conscientious clerk. He did all the paperwork on time and correctly. Sometimes he drove Mike up the wall, but Mike knew he would be lost without Badger.

Chapter 11
Harrisburg, Pennsylvania
June 14

June 18 was approaching faster than Ms Jessica Beck would have liked it to. She would have loved another week to double-check that all her i's were dotted and t's crossed, but she didn't have that kind of luck. What had started off as a social studies question-and-answer project for her class had turned into the community event of the season. Not really, but it seemed that way to her.

After the IEP meetings with Principal, Elaine Stone and the special needs teacher, Ms Theresa McBrian, Jessica could put all her energy into helping her students get organized and ready with their questions for the veterans. But Elaine asked Jessica if she could stick around for a few minutes. Elaine wanted to discuss something.

"How's your veterans' project going?" asked Elaine.

"It's turning into quite an event."

Event? This wasn't an event, Jessica thought. It was a question-and-answer project she put together to keep her students interested in their last social studies project of the school year.

"It's just a class project," Jessica said, "something a little different to keep my kids engaged and interested in social studies."

Jessica wasn't sure where this conversation was heading. But she had known Elaine long enough to tell when the wheels in her head were spinning and she had come up with a crazy idea. The phone rang. *Oh, thank goodness*, Jessica thought: *saved by the bell.*

Elaine picked up the phone. "Hello, Seamus." So, it was Assistant Superintendent Seamus Kelly. Jessica didn't think it would be polite to eavesdrop on their conversation. She excused herself and went to wait outside Elaine's office. On her way out, she noticed the ficus tree in the corner. A healthy ficus will stand tall with a grayish trunk and big, sturdy green leaves that can be used as hand fans on a hot summer day. This ficus, however, was in sad shape. First, it was by the door of Elaine's office, not getting any sun, and who knew the last time it had been watered? Its leaves were drooping, and most of them had turned bright yellow, which was a clear indication the poor tree needed water. The saddest part for the tree was that the watering can was inches away. If the tree could talk, it would probably scream, "Elaine, the way you are enjoying your coffee right now, I would really enjoy a drink of water… just sayin'." Jessica walked out the door and down the main hallway to see if she could find a custodian to open the supply closet, which had a sink large enough to fit the watering can.

By the time Jessica returned to Elaine's office with the watering can, Elaine was off the phone.

"Do you know you are the only one that waters that plant," Elaine said.

"No kidding?" Jessica answered. "First, it's not a plant. It's a tree. If this poor tree has any chance of surviving it should be in my living room where it will get the proper sunlight and attention it needs."

"I was going to take it home with me," Elaine said, "at the end of the school year."

"With all due respect, you are a great principal and good friend," Jessica said. "But the only way you would have a green thumb would be if you went to the art room and dipped your thumbs in green paint."

Both women started to laugh. It was late in the day, late in the school year, and a little joking back and forth between boss and employee was fine.

After Jessica watered the ficus, she and Elaine sat on the brown leather couch in Elaine's office. Elaine had two bottles of water and a bag of kettle corn they could munch on.

"Jessica," Elaine said, "I want you to know how wonderful the project you are doing with the kids is."

"Thank you," Jessica replied. "Why do I think there is more to this conversation than just a compliment?"

"There is," Elaine said. "But the compliment is genuine, and I sincerely meant it."

Jessica had never questioned Elaine's honesty or sincerity and wouldn't start now.

"Here is what I am thinking," Elaine said. "Instead of having the veterans come and talk just to your class, they could talk to the third, fourth and fifth-grade classes. We can do it in the auditorium. Your class could sit on one side of the stage and the veterans on the other, facing each other."

Emerson was an older school. It had a real auditorium with a stage and theater seats, the kind you had to hold down until you sat or they would snap back up into the folded position.

Jessica looked at Elaine as if she had grown a second head. The shock of what Elaine had suggested left Jessica speechless. She had known from Elaine's tone that she had something on her mind, but not this. It was a huge undertaking trying to get students to write their papers, getting questions ready to ask the veterans, and asking the veterans to come in and talk to the kids. Never mind doing it in front of the rest of the school.

"This was something to keep my kids interested in their final social studies project," Jessica said. "I didn't plan on getting the rest of the school involved."

"Why not?" Elaine asked. "This is a great opportunity for fourth and fifth graders to learn about history, as well, and great exposure for the school. I plan on inviting the mayor and a reporter from one of the newspapers, maybe both of them. I'm waiting to hear back from the editors."

"Don't tell me," Jessica said. "We are going to be serving refreshments, too."

"I called Swan Catering this morning, and put an order in for a cold cut platter, cheese platter, and pastries," Elaine said.

"This was supposed to be a fun, end-of-the-year project for my class," Jessica said. "Now we have reporters and a caterer. I have four days to put this together. Good thing I have the weekend to move and not leave a forwarding address."

Of course, she was joking, but she was taken aback by what Elaine was planning. This was a lot to do at the last minute. Still, it was a big deal for the school, so Jessica would do her best to make it all happen.

***

Kandahar, Afghanistan
June 15

In order to get Scott home for Jimmy's big day at school, Mike might have to stretch the truth with his bosses. He had a plan to send Scott to Washington, and he hoped it would all work out.

"Badger," Mike yelled. "For the love of all that's good and holy, what is taking so long to get HQ on the phone?"

"Sorry, sir," Badger answered. "It seems the satellite signal isn't strong enough at the moment to put the call through. I'm doing everything I can."

Patience was never a virtue of Mike's. The longer he waited, the more annoyed he got. He wasn't even sure if this was going to work. He planned to inform his bosses that as a matter of national security, it would be imperative to have a face-to-face meeting about the extremists rather than send information over the internet or the phone. The information his scouts had gathered was too sensitive to risk getting intercepted by the enemy.

If they agreed to the face-to-face meeting, the rest of the plan would be smooth sailing. He would just have to figure out what day and time Scott would have to leave to be in Washington on or about the seventeenth and make it to Harrisburg by the eighteenth. The time difference drove him crazy. He could never remember if they were eight and a half hours ahead or behind the United States or what day it was, yesterday, tomorrow, or next Tuesday. The whole thing made his head spin, but he would make it work. He had to make it work. He would rather not have another "dream" or "visit" from Julia. She was a nice little girl, but if he saw her again, he would question his sanity and wonder if he was mentally fit to command anything but his senses, if he even had control of those.

"Sir, sir," Badger yelled from his desk, "pick up the phone. I finally got HQ. It's General Clifton."

"It's about time," Mike said. "Lazy pencil pushers, they think once they make general they don't have to do anything, not even pick up the phone."

Mike waited a second before he answered the phone. He needed to calm down. He didn't want the general to hear how aggravated Mike was at how long it had taken to get through to Washington.

"Hello, General Clifton, sir," Mike said.

"What's the latest news on the enemy's position?" General Clifton asked.

"We believe we have a good handle on what is going on, and I would like to brief you on it. However, what concerns me, sir, is that the satellite signal keeps cutting in and out. We have gathered sensitive information, but it could be intercepted because of the weak signal. That's a risk we shouldn't take. I am suggesting a face-to-face meeting in Washington."

"Good thinking," the general said. "Send your team leader. Make sure he is here ASAP."

"Yes, sir," Mike said.

With that, the general hung up. Mike couldn't believe the way things had worked out. It was almost too easy, but he wasn't going to question it. He had stressed over how he would bring up to HQ the idea of sending Scott to hand deliver the information, so Scott could then get to Jimmy's school, yet somehow it had all worked out, at least the part about getting Scott to Washington. Mike was a hardened soldier. He had been to war, seen good friends die on the battlefield, but he had a soft spot when it came to Scott. Mike would never forget the day Scott had saved his little boy's life. Mike's wife, Jane, had just picked their son up from school, and they were on their way to get Mike from the base because his car was in the shop. Jane had said she would be at the base to get him around four o'clock. Mike looked at this watch. It was 4.10 p.m. Jane was usually very punctual, but Mike didn't think anything of her being late. Maybe she had stopped to talk to someone at the school, or there was traffic. Then the phone rang in his office, the scariest call he could have ever received.

The Harrisburg Police told him his wife and son had been in an accident and he needed to go to Carlisle Regional right away. He was terror-stricken. He couldn't move from his chair, let alone drive to the hospital. Scott walked into Mike's office to ask him something and saw the condition Mike was in. He asked Scott to drive him to the hospital. The accident Mike's wife had been involved in was horrific. She had got caught between two other drivers in a road-rage incident. One of the drivers had hit the front right quarter panel of her Jeep. According to the police report, she was hit with such force that she crossed into the left lane, went over the Jersey Barrier, and into the Sixth Street northbound, where the Jeep landed on its roof and was hit by an oncoming car.

When Scott and Mike arrived at the hospital, they went straight to the emergency room. They were met by a team of doctors, who informed Mike that his son had a serious head injury and had lost a lot of blood. They were prepping him for surgery but had to wait because the hospital had a shortage of AB positive blood. Scott told the doctors he was O negative and could donate to any blood type. As far as Mike was concerned, that day, Scott had saved his little boy's life.

Badger knocked on Mike's office door.

"Excuse me, sir," Badger said. "I need your signature on the daily reports."

"Tell Scooter I want to see him, ASAP," Mike said. "And put in for a request for a plane."

Chapter 12
Kandahar, Afghanistan
June 15

Mike went over to the mess hall to get a cup of coffee and a piece of cake or a doughnut. He had been on the phone with HQ for so long that he had missed lunch. He didn't feel like eating a meal, but he could have gone for a Boston cream or a raspberry jelly-filled doughnut with powdered sugar. He loved jelly doughnuts. They were his favorite, but more of the sugar went onto his uniform than into his mouth. As much as he loved being one of the guys, he was still in command. It was against protocol to have a dirty uniform when you were in charge. He was a firm believer in leading by example, especially when it came to how he appeared to his men.

As he was headed back to his tent, he heard the humming sounds of rotor blades to the east. Two Apache helicopters were heading toward the landing pad. He had forgotten all about the meeting Scott and his crew had with the British troops in Helmand Province to exchange information they had gathered about the extremists. England was one of America's closest allies, and Scott was exchanging information with the British to put a plan into action to stop the extremists' warehouse shenanigans.

Mike walked into the office's reception area with his coffee in his right hand and a jelly doughnut in his left. He had an iron will when it came to accomplishing a goal, but he had the spine of a jellyfish when it came to jelly doughnuts.

"Oh, sir," Badger said. "I looked for Scott all over the base. Then I remembered he and his crew had a meeting over in Helmand Province."

"They just landed," Mike replied. "Tell Scott I need to see him on the double."

"Yes, sir."

Scott was such a stickler for procedure that it would be fifteen or twenty minutes before he got to Mike's office. Mike had gone on missions with Scott in the past and was well aware Scott was going to make sure every knob and switch was turned off, and every pin that needed to be installed was. Then he would walk around the helicopter at least twice to make sure it was in perfect condition. Since Scott was going to be busy checking and double-checking his helicopter, Mike decided to enjoy his coffee and doughnut in peace. With any luck, Badger wouldn't come crashing through the door with something of utmost importance. Everything was always of utmost importance in Badger's mind. But as much as Badger drove Mike crazy with all the "yes sir" and "no sir," Mike depended on him.

The door to Mike's office was open. Scott was about to walk in without knocking. Mike was deep in thought. Instead of walking in quietly, Scott decided to pound on the office door to see if it would make Mike jump. He did and he spilled his coffee.

"Can't you knock quietly," Mike asked, "instead of pounding like you had dysentery and every latrine in camp was in use? Show a little respect. I'm still your boss."

Mike didn't mind practical jokes at his expense or banter with his men when it was all in good fun. But even when he was a little kid, he had hated when someone snuck up on him to scare him on purpose. He didn't want anyone to do that to him.

"How was the doughnut?" Scott answered Mike's question with a question of his own. "Did you manage to get any sugar in your mouth, or did your uniform enjoy it all?"

"Sit down, wise guy, before I change my mind and I go instead."

"Go?" Scott asked. "Go where?"

"I talked to HQ earlier today," Mike said. "They want the information we gathered about the extremists to be delivered to them personally. They don't want to take a chance on me sending it over the internet."

"So what does that have to do with me?" Scott asked.

"Your plane leaves in ten minutes."

Scott and his crew had been on a scouting mission, and they'd flown to the Helmand Province and met with the British. Now, Scott looked confused and was waiting for an answer. Mike took his sweet time cleaning up the coffee that Scott had made him spill.

"What are you talking about?" Scott asked. "Where am I going in ten minutes, or should I say eight minutes because you are cleaning up the coffee you spilled?"

"You're going to Washington," Mike said. "You know the place where we take orders from? That's where. Since when do you ask so many questions?"

"I can't just leave," Scott said.

Mike had thought Scott would have been glad to leave for a few days, even to go to Washington. Instead, this had turned into a game of twenty questions.

"You can, and you will. You now have seven minutes to get on the plane. I suggest you throw some clothes in your duffle bag and get moving."

"Okay, good, nothing like having time to plan," Scott said. "I'll see you when I get back. I am coming back, aren't I?"

"You bet your life you are," Mike said. "Dismissed."

"I'll see you when I see you." Scott saluted Mike and headed out the door.

But just as Scott left, Mike called him back.

"Oh, by the way," Mike said. "I've arranged for you to have a couple of days R&R while you're there. Go and see Jimmy."

"Roger that," Scott said. "Wait, what?"

Scott had said "Roger that" before he'd really heard what Mike had said.

"Did you say go see Jimmy?" Scott repeated it in case he hadn't heard Mike correctly.

"Yes, I did," Mike said. "Now you have five minutes before the plane leaves."

"Copy that."

***

Joint Base Andrews
June 15

Scott was awakened by Senior Airman Max Shaw shaking his shoulder.

"Sergeant," Max said. "Sergeant Andrews." This time, he said it in a deep, assertive voice, but not loud enough to scare Scott.

Scott looked around. He wasn't quite awake and not exactly sure where he was.

"We are approaching Andrews. You have been asleep for most of the flight."

"What time is it?" Scott asked. "What day is it for that matter?"

"Zero eight hundred on Friday, 15 June," Max answered.

"Can't be. I already had a 0800 on 15 June."

"Yes, you did. That was yesterday in Kandahar. It's today in Washington."

"I guess it is," Scott said. "Can't wait to cash in all those frequent flyer miles, compliments of Uncle Sam."

"Roger that," Max answered. "You and me both. The way I see it, I should have enough miles saved up to take me to the International Space Station. Twice."

The two men laughed as they prepared for the plane to touch down. Scott was still baffled at how Mike was able to get him to Washington, but really happy Mike had done it.

As the plane finished taxiing and came to a stop, Scott stood up to stretch his back and get the blood circulating. He wanted a cup of coffee and a shower before he headed over to the Pentagon. He was hoping the meetings with the Joint Chiefs of Staff wouldn't last all weekend. If they didn't, he might be able to go home and see Jimmy and spend more time with him. If not, he was going to show up at school on Monday morning and surprise Jimmy. Scott was going to play it by ear and see what happened with the meeting.

Ralph Waldo Emerson Elementary School
Harrisburg, Pennsylvania
June 18
7.30 a.m.

The big day for Ms Jessica Beck and her third-grade class was finally here. She arrived at school later than she would have liked. She was stuck in traffic and detoured from Crooked Hill Road to Shutt Mill Road due to a water main break that had happened overnight. She was nervous about today. But she wasn't going to get upset because of the traffic. It could not have been avoided, so she rolled with it.

She was happy and relieved that on Friday she had asked the afternoon custodial staff to set up the stage in the auditorium. That was one less thing she had to worry about now. She had asked them to put the chairs for her class and the podium for her on the right side of the stage and the chairs for the veterans on the left side.

She hoped her students remembered to wear red, white, and blue. The idea was for the kids to show patriotism for themselves, the school, and of course, the veterans. She was proud to be American and not afraid to express it—especially because of her older brother, Matt, and the special bond they had. She was excited to see him later that morning and happy he had taken time off to spend with her students.

Once she got to her classroom, the morning went by quickly. Usually by the time the kids went to their lockers and put their lunch boxes and backpacks away, their morning work was posted on the board and worksheets in the bin, but not today. She greeted her students as they entered the classroom and headed towards their seats. She thought they looked like flags swaying in the wind. All of them were dressed in red, white, and blue. Two of the girls, Melanie and Anna, had temporary American flag tattoos on their cheeks. Rosemarie, Stephanie, and Shelly had red-white-and-blue hair ribbons. The boys didn't fall behind the girls in showing their patriotism, either. Mikey had gotten a crew cut and had a flag designed on the side of his head. Ms Beck couldn't believe it.

Any nervousness or apprehension she felt about today disappeared. She looked at her class from her desk and couldn't remember feeling prouder to be a teacher. She wanted to tell her class how proud she was. Her eyes started to well up. She tried not to cry as she said good morning to them.

She looked at the time on the wall clock and rang the bell on her desk. This was her way of telling her class they should finish up the math problem they had been working on. Once they were finished, they would take their place on the blue carpet and sit with their legs folded and hands in their laps. They had sat that way every day since September and waited for the morning messages that came over the intercom.

"Good morning, boys and girls," Ms Beck said. "You look so sharp and so patriotic."

The kids had beaming smiles on their faces.

"I think you should each give the person sitting next to you a high five and tell them how good they look."

As they settled down, she saw Tina's hand go up.

"Yes, Tina," Ms Beck said.

"I'm so nervous about talking to the veterans," Tina said. "Suppose I forget what I want to ask them?"

"It's okay to be nervous," Ms Beck answered her. "It can be scary going up in front of so many people and talking to someone you never met before. Don't worry. The whole class is going to be there. I have all the questions written out on index cards for you. Everyone will have them in their hands, so you won't have to remember. Just read them off the cards."

The kids all let out sighs of relief. Billy stood up and shouted, "Thank you, Lord. I didn't think I was going to make it."

Ms Beck smiled and shook her head. Billy was one of her more animated students, so she wasn't surprised at his outburst.

"Okay, boys and girls. Let's head back to your desks, take out your English workbooks, and get started on the next page where you left off. It's going to be a fun day with a few surprises, I'm sure."

Chapter 13

RALPH WALDO EMERSON ELEMENTARY SCHOOL
Presents
Ms Beck's Third Grade Veterans Question and Answer Program

John Braddock .... Mayor
Eileen Stone .... Principal

Pledge of Allegiance .... Boys Scout Troop 51
National Anthem Harrisburg High School Marching Band
Welcome   Eileen Stone
Introduction of Veterans................ Jessica Beck
Major Matthew Beck .... U.S. Army
Chief Petty Officer Bradley Hager......... U. S. Navy
Captain Anne Marie Johnson .... U.S. Air Force
Lieutenant Max Walker .... U.S. Marines
Commander Nancy Witherspoon .... .U.S. Coast Guard

Ms Beck's Classroom
9.15 a.m.

Ms Beck was nervous, happy, worried, and excited all at the same time. The kids were settled in and working in their English workbooks. Since more people than she had initially expected would be attending this event, she would need help getting organized. She had asked Eileen if she could have Mrs Flynn, a teacher's assistant, come to her class between nine and nine fifteen to help her get her students started on their work, bring them down to the auditorium at nine forty-five, and get them settled into their seats on stage.

In the meantime, she would be at the main entrance with Elaine to greet the veterans, the mayor, and journalists from the local newspapers. As she approached the main entrance, she couldn't believe what she was seeing. She was at a loss for words, and her eyes started to well up with tears of happiness. The reception area looked fantastic. There was a beautiful three-dimensional flag welcome banner, which gave the illusion of waving in the wind. In addition, there were stand-up banners that had to be at least six feet high, one for each branch of the Armed Services. They looked like honor guards standing at attention by the entrance of the auditorium.

Mr John Simmons was the art teacher at Emerson. He had only been there two years, so he was still considered new to the school. However, he was not new to teaching art, which he had been doing for twenty-five years, mainly in high schools. He'd wanted a change of scenery and age group and came to Emerson. Now, he wanted to do his part and help Jessica with her event, so he had decorated the entryway.

"Thank you," Jessica said to Eileen. "This looks amazing."

"Don't thank me," Eileen answered. "This was all John's work. He heard about your question-and-answer day and wanted to decorate the lobby but didn't want you or anyone else to know about it."

"Why?" Jessica asked.

Eileen shrugged. "You'll have to ask him."

Jessica looked to see if she had time to find John. She had about eight minutes to spare, so down the hallway she went.

She reached John's classroom and knocked on the door. This was his prep time, so he didn't have any students.

"Good morning, Jessica," he said. "Come in."

"I can only stay a minute," she said. "I wanted to thank you for the beautiful banners you made for my kids' program."

"You're very welcome," John said. "I'm glad you liked them."

"I did very much. It was a wonderful surprise. I know the veterans will like them, as well."

John gave her a half-smile. He had a sad look in his eyes. She wanted to ask him if something was wrong, but she didn't have the time.

John was a veteran of the Navy. He had served on the USNS Comfort, a hospital ship that took care of soldiers injured during combat. Not many people knew that he had served, and he preferred it that way. He was very proud of his service, but he didn't want to talk about it. He didn't want people to ask him questions about what he had seen or what soldiers went through. It was too emotional for him. He just filed it away and went about his life.

"I have to head back down to the lobby," Jessica said. "If you don't have a class coming in, why don't you join us in the auditorium? Afterwards, the veterans can thank you in person for the way the lobby looks."

"No thanks necessary," John answered. "But I would like to come and sit in the back if that's okay."

"Of course it's okay," Jessica said. "My brother is coming, too. I'll introduce you to him." They reached the main hallway. John continued to the auditorium. Jessica stayed back. The cafeteria staff had finished setting up tables with coffee pots and pastries. She had known refreshments and lunch would be served later, but she hadn't known that Elaine had asked the cafeteria staff to have coffee ready. Jessica smiled. She was lucky to work in such a great school.

Just then, someone tapped her shoulder. When she turned, it was Matthew. Ever since she was a little girl, she and Matt had always been the best of friends. She idolized her older brother. Although they talked once a week, they hadn't seen each other since Christmas. She gave him the biggest hug she could.

"I'm so glad you're here," Jessica said. "It's good to see you."

"Would I ever let you down?" Matt asked. "It's good to see you, too."

"I wish Patti could have been here."

Patti was Matt's wife. She and Jessica had been best friends ever since they met when Jessica was a little girl and Patti was working at Top This. Since then, her brother had started his own ice cream company. Patti was vice president and in charge of marketing and promotions, as well. It was difficult for her to take time off. Jessica was resigned to her not being there, but as she was letting go of her brother, she blinked. No, it couldn't be. But it was. Patti was standing to the left of Matthew.

"Oh my goodness," Jessica said. "What a wonderful surprise."

"When Matt told me he was coming," Patti said, "I told him your sister has always supported me. Now it's my turn to support her. Here I am. I wanted to surprise you. I told him not to tell you."

So much was happening. Men and women in uniform, both past and present soldiers, filled the lobby. Ms Beck couldn't believe her small class project had turned into such a huge patriotic event.

Coming down the hallway right on time was her class. She couldn't thank Mrs Flynn, the teacher's assistant, enough for taking over so Ms Beck could be at the main entrance to greet everyone. She was excited to see her class all dressed in red, white, and blue. Sometimes her class grated on her nerves, but she loved every one of her kids.

Everyone was shuffling into the auditorium and finding seats. Her class found its way up to the stage. So did the five veterans who each represented one of the service branches.

After the national anthem, the auditorium lights dimmed, the stage lights went up, and Mrs Stone addressed the crowd.

"Good morning. I am Elaine Stone, principal of Emerson Elementary. I would like to welcome you to our school. I would like to take credit for putting this fantastic event together, but I can't. This is all happening because of the hard work of Ms Jessica Beck and her third-grade class, and the only credit I can take is for hiring Ms Beck many years ago. I am so glad I did. Now, I am going to turn the microphone over to her."

"Thank you, Mrs Stone. Good morning and welcome." Ms Beck began her part of the program. "Thank you not only for your service but for helping to make my students' last project of the year so interesting and educational. They had a lot of fun researching the different branches of our military. Some of them have told me they might even want to join when they get older. Our first interviewer is going to be Stephanie, and she did her report on the Coast Guard."

Stephanie was one of Ms Beck's friendlier students. She was a true believer in the idea that anything a boy can do, a girl can do better. She was opinionated, stubborn, and yet had a heart of gold. Her strong exterior was a defense mechanism so that no one could get to her heart. Even at a young age, she was protecting herself from being hurt. The summer between Stephanie's first- and second-grade year, Stephanie's mother had decided she didn't want to be married any more and walked out on Stephanie and her father. Stephanie had therefore learned at a young age to protect herself, and yet she was the first student to volunteer to help a teacher or comfort a classmate if they had gotten hurt.

"Okay," Stephanie said. "My question is for Commander Witherspoon."

Commander Witherspoon was her grandmother's next-door neighbor. Stephanie had known her ever since she was a baby.

"How old were you when you thought about joining the Coast Guard? Were your parents happy or sad? Do you always have to wear your hair in a bun?"

"All good questions, Stephanie," Commander Witherspoon said. "Okay, where do I start? I was a little older than most people when I joined. I was twenty-two and almost out of college. I wasn't sure what I wanted to do with my life except that I wanted to travel and see different and exciting things. As for my parents, I grew up in foster care with my older brother. I really didn't know my parents, but my brother was worried for me and proud of me at the same time."

"I don't have a mom either," Stephanie said, interrupting the commander. "My dad is proud of me."

"I am positive he is," Commander Witherspoon said, reassuring her. "As for my hair, it has to be in a boring bun when I am on duty, but I do get to let it down, and I wear makeup and do my nails when I'm off work."

"Really, you can?" Stephanie perked up. "Okay, maybe I might want to join when I get older now."

Everyone in the audience started to laugh. Stephanie turned to go back to her seat. Ms Beck helped Stephanie down from the step stool behind the podium.

"Thank you, Commander Witherspoon and Stephanie," Ms Beck said. "Our next interviewer is Mikey. He did his report on the Army."

Mikey was a neat kid, Ms Beck thought. He was friendly, polite, and funny and always wanted to learn new things from a teacher or a classmate.

He waited until the audience stopped applauding before he started to speak.

"My question is for Major Beck," he said. "I have two questions, maybe three. Ms Beck told us you are her older brother. I have a younger sister, and she is a pain in the butt. Was Ms Beck a pain in the butt, and how long do I have to wait for my sister to stop being such a pain in the butt?"

Everyone in the auditorium broke out into laughter. Mikey didn't realize he was funny. He truly wanted advice from one older brother to another.

"My second question is, were you in a war, and were you afraid you wouldn't come home alive?"

Suddenly the audience that had been laughing a few moments ago turned silent and serious. Mikey's questions were a harsh reminder of the risk military families lived with. For the men and women in the military and their families, war wasn't something they watched on television. They had to learn how to deal with it every day.

"Well, Mikey," Major Beck said. "Let me answer your second question first. Yes, I've been to war. When your teacher was a little girl, I had to leave and go to a place called Bosnia. A lot of bad things were happening there, and they needed the United States to help out. We went and helped and did the best job we could."

He looked at Jessica. She had tears in her eyes. He knew how much his little sister loved him. He winked at her, just as he always did when the white bus drove away whenever he was deployed. That was their secret signal that he was going to come back and for her not to worry.

"Yes, Mikey," Matt continued, "there is always a fear one of us might not come back alive, but we use that fear to keep us sharp and focused. Because more than anything, we want to come home. To answer your first question, was your teacher a pain in the butt? No, she was always my best friend. In time, you will actually like your sister as well."

"Best friend?" Mikey said. "No thanks; who wants a sister for a best friend? Not me."

Once again, everyone in the audience started to laugh

Chapter 14
Washington, D.C.
The Pentagon

On the plane from Afghanistan to Washington, Scott had planned how things would go when the meeting was over. He would go back to his hotel room, order room service for dinner, watch TV and relax. The next day, he would wake up at 0615, take a shower, order room service for breakfast, and get on the road to Harrisburg to surprise Jimmy.

Scott didn't get back to his hotel room until twelve thirty. He was physically and mentally exhausted. The meeting with General Gailey and the rest of the Pentagon's high-ranking officers had run much longer than he expected. He thought it would last three hours. It lasted six.

None of his plans worked out. Now, his cell phone woke him up. It was General Gailey. He needed Scott to be back at the Pentagon by 0800 to go over a few things. It never bothered Scott to change plans that only involved himself, but he didn't want to disappoint Jimmy. At least Jimmy didn't know Scott was two hours away. At the same time, he felt terrible because Mike had gone to so much trouble to get him there. Scott was going to do his best to see Jimmy, even for five minutes.

After another hour and a half, the meeting was finally wrapping up. By the time all the last-minute chit-chat and saluting was done, more time has passed. Scott looked at this watch. He couldn't believe it was ten forty-five. He shook his head in annoyance. By now, he should either have been at Jimmy's school or at least pulling into the parking lot. Instead, he was still in Washington because the general had to recap a meeting that happened less than eight hours ago. This just solidified Scott's belief in how useless West Point graduates were. You told a field soldier once what the plan was, and they got it. You could tell a West Point graduate something in triplicate, and they still wouldn't understand it.

"Anything wrong, sergeant?" General Gailey asked, startling Scott. "You do know these meetings don't have a time limit."

"Nothing's wrong, sir."

Scott could tell by the tone in the general's voice that he was not happy with Scott.

"Colonel Cullen and I had a conversation early this morning," the general continued. "Seems you wanted to go and see your brother in Harrisburg if you had time after the meeting?"

"Yes, sir, if I had time," Scott said. "Colonel Cullen had arranged for some R&R for me while I was here. Now that the meeting is over, since Harrisburg is only two hours away, I was going to rent a car and drive up to see him for a few hours, drive back, jump on a C-5 to Kabul, and report back to base."

One of the clerks interrupted Scott. "Rent a car and drive to Harrisburg today?"

"Yes, why?" Scott said. "Do they not rent cars on Sundays?"

"The interstate is shut down and will be for a few hours," the clerk said. "According to the news, there is a fifteen-car pileup. Someone cut off a tanker truck full of oil, it landed on its side, and it's spilling oil all over the road. If that wasn't bad enough, a truck carrying dairy cows was hit, and the cows got out of the truck and are running all over the road as well."

Scott didn't know whether he wanted to start laughing or start swearing. Ordinarily, he was an even-tempered person and took everything in his stride, except when it came to Jimmy. Scott missed his little brother and really wanted to see him. Scott knew he would never make it to Jimmy's school to see his fellow veterans speak. He was giving up on the idea of going to Harrisburg at all. Accidents happened. The oil spill was messy and dangerous, and people could have been hurt. But cows? Really?? If he were to tell Mike that he didn't get to go and see Jimmy because cows had gotten loose on the interstate, he would never hear the end of it. In fact, Scott knew what Mike would say.

"Cows?" Mike would say. "You don't say. The truck driver should have mooooved over to the other lane to avoid getting hit." Or, "Don't try to milk us for sympathy because you didn't see Jimmy." Mike and his bad puns made Scott crazy.

Scott might try taking the train to Harrisburg. If a car took two hours, how much longer would a train take? The more Scott thought about not seeing Jimmy, the angrier he got at the general. He still could spend a few hours on Monday with Jimmy after school. But if General Gailey had understood everything Scott was trying to tell him about the extremists the night before, there wouldn't have been another meeting this morning. He could have left Washington early, avoided the oil spill and the cows. He was so close and yet so far. He walked over to the clerk's desk to see if he could get information about the train. General Gailey was talking to the clerk, probably about nothing. Scott wasn't sure if the clerk would know anything about the train schedule. If she didn't, perhaps she could look it up on the internet for him. He waited until they stopped talking.

"Excuse me," Scott said. "Would you by chance happen to know how long it would take to get to Harrisburg by train and when is the next train leaving?"

"One moment." The clerk pulled up the Amtrak schedule. "Seems it will take four hours on the express train."

"Hmm, a little longer than I thought," Scott said. "Thank you, ma'am. I appreciate you looking."

Scott felt so many different things. He was angry with the general, disheartened that he couldn't rent a car and that the train would take so many hours to get to Harrisburg. Mostly, he was disappointed that he might not be able to see Jimmy for as long as he would have liked.

He would have bet his house Mike probably had called in every favor anyone owed him to get Scott to Washington. Scott was about to go back to his hotel room and check his emails, see if Mike had contacted him, and figure out what to do the rest of his day and night. As he turned, General Gailey looked at him. Scott wanted nothing to do with the general. He was the reason Scott wouldn't see Jimmy until he got his orders to come home.

"Sergeant," the general said, "you win some and you lose some. Today you lost. Tomorrow you will be on a plane heading back to the base, and this will all become a memory. Go catch a movie; you will feel better."

If a moment ago Scott disliked the general, now Scott pretty much hated the guy. He really was a cold-hearted horse's behind, Scott thought.

"Thanks for the suggestion, sir." Scott walked away in disgust. As he did, he caught the clerk rolling her eyes at the general's comment. That made him smile and lightened his mood a little bit. It seemed she wasn't a fan of General Gailey either.

"Smart girl," he thought. *"Kinda pretty. Long brown hair, deep brown eyes, great smile. She doesn't wear a lot of makeup, but she's really cute."*

Scott went back to his hotel room utterly frustrated. Was he mad at the cows on the highway, the general, the war, or just the fact that he wouldn't see his younger brother? It was a combination of everything. Until he could figure out what to do, he would watch TV and maybe fall asleep for a couple of hours.

No such luck! Twenty minutes into watching TV, he'd fallen asleep, but his phone woke him up.

"Sergeant Andrews," Scott said. He always answered the phone that way. Rarely did he ever get a phone call. He was more of a texter than a talker.

"Sergeant Andrews," a woman said. "This is Erika Clark, the clerk at the Pentagon that looked up the Amtrak schedule for you earlier."

"Oh yes. Hi," Scott replied. "How can I help you?"

"Oh no," she said. "It's me that can help you."

"I'm sorry, Erika, I'm not following you."

"Can you come back here as soon as possible? I have come up with an idea to get you to Harrisburg."

Scott needed a few seconds to get his wits about him.

"Sure, Erika," he answered. "I will be there in ten minutes."

"See you then." She hung up the phone.

For the second time today, the phone had woken him, and for the second time, he was headed back to the Pentagon. He rushed to put his uniform shirt back on, brush his hair and his teeth. He grabbed his watch, and out the door he went. So much for relaxing.

Within a few minutes, Scott arrived at the Pentagon again. If he never saw that place again, he wouldn't miss it. He wasn't sure where to go or even why he was there. He only really knew where the conference room was. He headed in that direction and would ask someone to find Erika if he had to. Luckily he didn't have to ask anyone; he saw her desk down the hallway to his left. There was no doubt this was the longest hallway he had ever seen or walked down. He had read the Pentagon had more than seventeen miles of hallways. He was convinced this hallway alone was at least seventeen miles long, but he finally reached her desk.

"Hello, Erika," Scott said. "I got here as soon as I could."

"Sergeant Andrews, already?" she said. "Wow, that was fast."

"I didn't want to keep you waiting. The sooner we figure out what the problem is, the sooner I can go back to my room and do nothing until I fly out tomorrow."

"Problem?" she said. "What problem?"

"The reason why I'm here."

"Oh, that," she said. "It has nothing to do with the meeting you had. It has to do with the traffic jam on the interstate."

"I'm sorry, I was half asleep when you called," Scott said. "Honestly, I don't remember what you said, just that I needed to be here ASAP."

"Well, the traffic delayed the supplies that were supposed to be driven down here and loaded onto the plane you were going to be on tomorrow."

"I still don't understand," Scott said. "Even if the supplies are delayed, they can get here by the time we fly out. The road will open again in a few hours."

"I'm sure it will, and things will get back to normal," she said. "However, we can't take the risk of another delay and decided to leave the supplies in Pennsylvania and have them fly out from there tomorrow."

"Umm, Erika, who is we?" Scott asked. "You can't change a delivery and a plane manifest, just like that." Scott snapped his fingers. "A certain protocol needs to be followed."

"You're right. Most people can't. But I can. I have the right connections."

"Okay, then. I will just step back and let you call your people."

He was baffled by this conversation and captivated by Erika. He liked her self-confidence and the way she took charge of things. Perhaps she knew more about protocol than he originally thought.

A deep booming voice behind Scott said hi to Erika. Scott turned and saw something that resembled a sequoia tree. This man had to be at least six-foot-six. Scott stood all of five-nine. Many men he worked with were taller than he was, and he was okay with that. But those men weren't like this man. If his height wasn't intimidating enough, he was a brigadier general. Scott snapped to attention and saluted.

"At ease, sergeant," the general said. "My daughter told me the supplies were delayed because cows got loose on the highway."

"Yes, sir," Scott said. "Begging your pardon, sir, did you say your daughter?"

"I did."

Erika couldn't stop grinning at the confusion on Scott's face.

"Sergeant Andrews," she said. "Allow me to introduce my father, Brigadier General Michael Clark. I told you I knew people and had connections."

Scott extended his hand. "It's a pleasure to meet you, sir."

"My daughter said that Gailey gave you a hard time about not being able to get to Harrisburg for something you had going on there."

"Yes, sir," Scott replied. "My little brother had a school function. I thought since I was here, if I had time, I would drive up to see him for about an hour and drive back down and get ready to leave tomorrow."

"Gailey and I went to the Academy together," General Clark said. "He is and always was a bag full of wind. The only combat he ever saw was in his kitchen when his wife would yell at him for not washing the dishes."

Scott tried not to laugh, but it didn't work. He chuckled.

"Sergeant, how long will it take you to gather up your gear and head to Andrews?"

"Twenty minutes, sir," Scott answered.

"Good, report back here in twenty minutes and we will arrange for someone to take you to Andrews for a flight up to Penna. You do know where Penna is, sergeant."

"Oh yes, sir, I do."

Penna National Guard was where Scott was stationed before his unit was deployed.

"Go and see your brother and report back to Penna at 0600 hours tomorrow morning for the flight back to your unit."

Scott once again shook the general's hand.

"I can't thank you enough, sir," Scott said.

"Yes, you can. Be safe out there and bring everyone in your unit home to their families."

"And thank you, Erika. You're awesome," Scott said. "I don't know how I can thank you for all of this, either."

"Oh, I know how," she said.

"Just name it."

"Take me out to dinner when you come home," she said.

Scott's jaw hit the top of his boots, and his face turned beet-red. He was a shy guy when it came to women. Her being so forward caught him off guard.

"Oh, okay," he said. "I will."

"If I give you my email address, would you write to me?" Erika said. "I'd like to know you made it back okay."

"Sure thing," Scott said. "I'll let you know."

Scott had to stop himself from running out of the Pentagon. He couldn't wait to get back to his room and gather up his gear. In a couple of hours, he was going to surprise his brother. Scott had always believed he would rather be lucky than good. He definitely felt that way now.

Joint Base Andrews
1230

Scott gathered his things and rushed back to the Pentagon. Erika had told him to meet her back at her desk so she could arrange a staff car to get him to Andrews. Scott was a no-nonsense, simple, straightforward, sensible person, especially when he wore his uniform. But Erika flustered him. He'd left Afghanistan not just to deliver confidential information, but because he wanted to see Jimmy. Somehow during all this, he'd ended up with a dinner date when he got home. It all happened so fast he couldn't make sense of it, but for the first time in his life, he didn't want it to make sense. So far, he liked what he saw in Erika. She was intelligent, quick on her feet, pretty, and she didn't seem to think much of General Gailey, either.

As he entered the building and walked down the long hallway with all the closed doors, it reminded him of the scene in *Willy Wonka and the Chocolate Factory* when the people were walking, looking for the entrance to the chocolate factory, and the hallway appeared to get smaller as they seemed to get bigger. He had to stop himself from laughing. He didn't think it would be dignified laughing in the Pentagon by himself. Erika's desk was ahead. However, he didn't see her there. She must be checking on something. Maybe she wasn't back from lunch yet, or she was getting a cup of coffee. Whatever the case was, he would sit in one of the chairs opposite her desk and wait for her.

He didn't have to wait long. As soon as he reached her desk, she came around the corner with a cup of coffee in her hand. Scott chuckled.

"What's so funny?" Erika asked.

"Nothing," Scott answered.

"Do you always laugh when you are by yourself?"

"Sometimes."

"Really," she said. "And the government trusts you with secrets?"

"Okay, I'll tell you. This place reminded me of the scene in Willy Wonka when all the people walked down the hallway. It appeared as if they were getting bigger and bigger, and the room was getting smaller and smaller."

"Oh, wonderful," Erika said, shaking her head. "And we trust you with guns and our freedom. I bet when you were a kid, you ran with scissors too."

"Nope," Scott answered. "But I did color outside the lines. I never followed instructions or like to be ordered around."

Erika stopped and looked at Scott. He was in the military. His entire adult life, he'd been ordered around by someone with a higher rank than his.

"Excuse me?" she said. "You don't like to be ordered around?"

Scott winked. He enjoyed teasing her. She was a good sport, and she teased him, too. He had to do something to try and calm his nerves. Teasing her was a good way of doing it.

"You have a plane to catch," Erika said. "I'd better get you out of here, or we will both get into trouble."

"Yes, ma'am," Scott answered.

Erika was on the phone making arrangements. Her father and General Gailey were walking down the hallway discussing something. She wanted to get Scott out of there as soon as she could, so Scott wouldn't have to deal with Gailey or his snide remarks. She wasn't fast enough. Here they came.

They stopped at Erika's desk to drop off the files they had in their hands. Scott stood and saluted them both.

"Sergeant," General Gailey said. "I told you there wouldn't be any way of going to see your brother, and I was right."

Scott wanted to give him a nasty response, but he knew he couldn't, so he would answer as respectfully as he could.

However, before Scott could answer, General Clark jumped in.

"At ease, general," General Clark said. "I told Sergeant Andrews to meet me here."

Scott loved the fact that not only did General Clark tower over General Gailey physically, but Clark outranked Gailey as well. So Gailey couldn't do anything more than back down and keep his mouth shut.

Erika interrupted the men to tell Scott the staff car would be outside the main entrance in five minutes.

Scott thanked Erika once again. He told her he would contact her for the dinner he promised her once he got home. He was usually reserved and quiet. He couldn't believe he'd promised to take Erika out to dinner in front of her father. It was very out of character, and she continued to fluster him. He turned towards the generals, saluted them, and left to catch the plane.

All he could think of now was how glad he would be to see Jimmy after all these months. He wasn't sure where he was going to meet up with him. Would he have enough time to catch him at school, or should he drive straight to his house? He wasn't going to worry about that. It would fall into place.

Scott was dropped off in front of the base and checked in with one of the airmen, who directed him to the tarmac where his plane was.

He headed over to the C-130 Hercules, which a group of soldiers was loading with various boxes. They stopped when they saw him. He introduced himself and asked if they needed any help. One of the soldiers looked confused. Scott was a sergeant. He outranked the corporals loading the plane.

"You want to help us?" the soldier asked as if he hadn't heard Scott correctly.

They weren't used to getting help from anyone, let alone being asked if they needed help, especially not by a superior officer.

"I know I've been out of the country a long time," Scott answered. "But I think I'm still speaking English."

"Yes, sergeant, you are. Just not used to someone that outranks us asking us if we need help."

"That's why I do it," Scott said. "I always lead from the front. I won't ever ask anyone to do something I wouldn't do myself. Remember that. It's how respect is earned and kept."

Also, the sooner they loaded everything, the sooner they could take off, and he would get to Harrisburg. It took about fifteen minutes to get everything into the plane and strapped down. The crew was in the cockpit of the aircraft doing safety checks. Scott was listening to the pilot and the flight engineer going over their checklist. He was such a stickler for safety. If they forgot something he would tell them, but he would also be careful not to step on anyone's toes. Right now, he was just hitching a ride because cows got loose on the highway.

The safety check was completed, and the crew was just about ready to go. Both pilots, along with the flight engineer, walked over to Scott and introduced themselves.

"Sergeant Andrews, I'm Captain David Boyd," the engineer said. "Friends call me Pink." He extended his hand.

"Pleased to meet you, Pink," Scott said. "Friends call me Scooter."

"Over there to the left is our co-pilot, Lieutenant Tim Parker, and the lazy one sitting down is Lieutenant Zack Ford."

Scott was perplexed as to why someone would have the nickname Pink. The guy stood about six-foot-one, not a bad-looking guy. He was around forty-five years old, with salt-and-pepper hair, a regulation military cut. He didn't have an ounce of fat on him. Pink was an interesting nickname. Scott was looking forward to hearing the story behind it. There had to be a story, just like there was one behind his nickname. When Scott was eighteen, he got a speeding ticket on his way back to the base and his sergeant never let him forget it.

"Hey, Pink," Lieutenant Parker called. "Time's a-ticking. We need to get in the air."

"Roger that."

Scott sat on one of the red seats with the mesh back against the plane's wall. He strapped himself in and waited to hear the click, click, click of the switches in the cockpit, the pilot getting clearance from the tower, the engines being switched on. He prepared for takeoff. No matter how many times Scott had taken off in a plane, it never got old. He had wanted to fly since he was six. Whether he was the pilot or a passenger, he loved being in the air.

He looked at his watch: 13.45. No way would Scott make it to Jimmy's school before he got out. He had missed Jimmy's special day at his school. He felt terrible, but he wasn't going to harp on that. He had tried, and if it wasn't for General Gailey, he would have made it. Well, he was going straight to Jimmy's house and spend time with him there. Maybe they would go and get something to eat. Whatever Jimmy wanted to do would he okay with him.

Scott was ready to fall asleep when Pink walked towards him.

"I didn't wake you?" Pink asked.

"No, sir," Scott replied.

"We are going to have a lot more cargo and men on the plane tomorrow," Pink said. "We are going to have to rearrange everything to add seats. One hundred fifty more men are being deployed, and I'm responsible for getting them to Afghanistan."

"Roger that," Scott said. "After I see my brother and spend some time with him, I can report back to the base early and help to load the supplies."

"I might take you up on that."

"Yes, sir. I'll be at the base by 0600, but if you need me earlier, I can be there."

"0600 works," Pink said.

"With all due respect, sir," Scott said, "do you mind if I ask how you got your nickname? I got mine because I had a bit of a lead foot when I was eighteen. I got a speeding ticket going back to the base."

Pink started laughing. "I remember when I was young and dumb. I got my nickname because of my twin sister," Pink said. "She was diagnosed with breast cancer when she was thirty-two. She had just given birth. She had twins, two little boys. They were handsome like their uncle.

"My sister was the toughest woman on the planet. She vowed she would beat the cancer, and nothing was going to take her away from her babies. She did everything she had to do, surgery, chemotherapy, you name it. At times she was so sick she couldn't move. She won that battle. Since then, I have had a pink ribbon sewn inside every uniform I own. Hey, I better get back. It's time to land."

"Yes, sir," Scott said.

Scott sat back in his chair. He thought about the story that Pink had just told him. He was in awe of how much Pink loved his sister and how highly he thought of her. The closest thing Scott had to a sister was Barbara, Jimmy's mother. He knew if she were diagnosed with cancer, she would fight just as hard as Pink's sister to beat it, for Jimmy's sake.

***

Ralph Waldo Emerson Elementary School
1:45

The veterans' question-and-answer program was a success. Everyone had a wonderful time. The lunch had been catered for the veterans, and the other guests were just wrapping up. Ms Beck breathed a big sigh of relief. She was so proud of her class. They'd done a great job asking the veterans questions and listening to their answers. Even the kids who didn't feel comfortable asking questions sat quietly and paid attention. She wasn't sure if she would ever do it again, but she was so happy she'd done this. Who was she kidding? She was already planning for next year, but with one change. She might not wait for the end of the school year. She might do it in late spring.

As she was saying goodbye to the last veteran, her brother, Jessica saw John and thanked him again for the fantastic decorations and introduced him to Matt. She left the two men to talk. Her students lined up in the hallway to head back to their classroom and get ready for dismissal.

Once they got to their classroom, before the kids started packing to go home, she told them to sit at their desks. Of course, that was met with a bunch of groans. They thought they were going to leave early.

"Class, settle down," Ms Beck said. "I wanted you to sit at your desks for a few minutes, so I can tell you how proud I am of every one of you. This wasn't an easy project I gave you, and I wasn't sure how it would turn out. Even my brother told me how impressed he was with you. I want to thank you for acting so grown up and making me so proud."

Stephanie raised her hand. "Ms Beck, I have a question."

"Yes, Stephanie?" Ms Beck answered.

"I know you won't be our teacher next year. This was a lot of fun, and I learned a lot. If you do this again, can the class I am in participate in asking the veterans more questions?"

Ms Beck had to bat her eyelashes a few times to fight back tears of joy. Her kids wanted to do this again.

"I will talk to Principal Stone about it," Ms Beck answered. "Let us see what we can come up with for next year."

The whole class started clapping, and some of the girls were cheering. How they could get their voices so high without hurting their throats was beyond Ms Beck. But she was happy.

"Okay, class, listen up. Quietly stand up and put your chairs on top of your desks and line up for dismissal."

The kids shuffled out of class. Whoever was riding the bus went down the hallway to the left. Whoever was getting picked up by a parent or riding a bike went to the right.

Jimmy usually took the bus home in the afternoon, but today he had asked his mom if she could pick him up. She had taken the day off because the plumber was coming over to fix the water heater. He saw his mom's car and waited for her to drive up to the spot where the kids were picked up from.

"Hi, Mom." Jimmy opened the car door.

"Hi, honey. How was your day? How did the question-and-answer program go?"

"It was a lot of fun," Jimmy said. "Ms Beck's older brother was there. He is a major in the Army. He told us all about Ms Beck when she was a little girl. He went to Brazil to fight a war when she was little."

"Brazil?" Jimmy's mom asked him. "Are you sure he said Brazil, honey?"

"Mom, I was there. I heard what he said. He said a lot of bad things were happening, and we had to go there and help out."

"Are you sure he didn't say Bosnia?" she asked.

"Oh yeah, that's it, Bosnia," Jimmy agreed. "I was almost right. Both countries start with a B."

As they made the left onto their street, they noticed a car in their driveway. "Who is parked in our driveway?" Jimmy asked.

"I don't know," Barbara said. "The plumber was here earlier, but he was in his work van. Whoever it is, I hope it's not any bad news."

"Maybe he forgot a tool or something," Jimmy said, "and on his way home, he came back to get it with his car."

As they drove towards the house, Scott was sitting on the front steps waiting for them.

"Mom, it's Scott," Jimmy screamed.

She stopped the car. Jimmy jumped out and ran straight into Scott's arms.

"Hey, buddy," Scott said.

Jimmy was without words; he was so happy to see his brother he wasn't ready to let go of him and talk to him.

Scott finally put Jimmy down from his bear hug, and he headed towards Jimmy's mom.

"Hey, Barbie Doll," Scott said.

"Hi Scott." She also gave him a big hug. "It's so good to see you. I'm glad you are home."

"I'm not home to stay," Scott said. "I'm going back tomorrow at 0600. Let's go inside, and I'll explain. I know you won't believe it."

Chapter 15
Jimmy's Home

Barbara unlocked the front door and let the boys go in first. Scott carried Jimmy piggyback from the front yard. He liked Jimmy's home. It always gave him an inviting, warm feeling. It had been built in 1918 and had a lot of charm. It was the tallest house in the neighborhood. It had a combination of stone and aluminum siding with light blue shutters on the bedroom windows. Scott was happy that Jimmy had a nice house to grow up in. He was also glad Jimmy had a more stable childhood than he did.

Scott's parents never got along. They were constantly arguing. He often wondered why they got married. When they finally got divorced, Scott didn't see his father very often. He traveled a lot. He was a supervisor at one of the steel mills in Pittsburgh, where Scott grew up. Scott lived with his mom near Harrisburg until he graduated from high school then joined the Army. It wasn't until his father met Barbara that he rebuilt his relationship with his father. When Jimmy was born, Scott felt as if he finally had a real family.

Jimmy was four-years-old when their father died coming home from a business trip. It had been snowing heavily that day. It was rush hour. Someone in a Jeep Renegade was driving way too fast. The cars in front of him were slowing down because of the snow that was accumulating on the road. The driver lost control of his vehicle. The Jeep rolled over. Trying to avoid getting hit or hitting someone else, Scott's father veered off the road and plunged down the embankment. From that day on, Scott promised Barbara that he and Jimmy would always be close, and he kept that promise.

As they entered the house, the dog greeted them. Bear was a well-behaved half-German shepherd, half-Labrador retriever rescue. He weighed sixty-five pounds, black with a little bit of tan on his chest, floppy ears, and a tail that was always wagging. Even though Scott had his own home about two miles from Jimmy's, this house was Scott's home away from home. He spent a lot of time playing video games with Jimmy in the wintertime when he couldn't fly as much due to the unpredictable weather.

They made their way down the hallway heading towards the kitchen. To the left was a beautiful formal living room. It gave the impression a person had stepped into a palace. It had a baby grand piano, mirrored walls, and a built-in doll showcase to show off the doll collection Barbara had started when she was six-years- old.

In the kitchen, Barbara went over to the coffee maker and emptied the grounds from that morning from the basket. She rinsed it out and scooped out coffee from a canister. Scott sat in the same place every time he visited, on the last seat to the right at the breakfast bar. Jimmy usually sat in the first seat, and Barbara remained standing on the other side of the counter. It was easier for her to hand them their plates or coffee cups that way.

"I have always loved walking into this house," Scott said. "Seeing this beautiful living room and how much time and effort you put into it does not make me want to go back to my tent in the desert any time soon."

"I can imagine," Barbara said. "It's just a shame you couldn't stay longer than a few hours."

"Are you sure you can't stay longer?" Jimmy jumped into the conversation.

"Sorry, buddy," Scott said. "You know I would if I could. I didn't even know I was coming back home until two days ago. I think it was two days ago. With all the traveling and meetings, I'm not sure what day it is. All I know is I have to be at the base tomorrow by 0600 to fly back to Afghanistan."

"Wait, what?" Jimmy said. "You were here yesterday?"

Jimmy's facial expression changed from cheerful to sad almost instantaneously.

Scott felt horrible seeing Jimmy's expression change that fast.

"I was in Washington yesterday," Scott said. "I had meetings at the Pentagon. I planned to leave Washington early this morning, but this general had to have another meeting this morning. There was an oil spill on the interstate, so they had to shut it down, then cows got loose. It was just a mess."

"If the general called for another meeting," Barbara said, "then it had to be important."

"No," Scott said. "He wanted to go over the plans one more time. He has to be the dumbest general in the Army.

I swear he couldn't find his way out of a tank with the hatch open."

Jimmy laughed so hard he spat his chocolate milk all over the counter and himself, which made Scott laugh.

"You had to wait until he had a mouthful of milk?" Barbara said.

"Timing is everything," Scott said, "when you are telling a joke."

"Since you think that was so funny," Barbara said, "you clean it up."

She threw the dish rag at Scott, and he caught it mid-air.

"It would be my pleasure," Scott said. "Just to see Jimmy laugh like that, it was worth it."

"Jimmy, go upstairs and change your shirt," Barbara said.

"Later, Mom," Jimmy said. "I want to hear more of the story."

"Hey now," Scott said. "You do what your mom tells you to do. Don't give her any grief. Just say yes, ma'am, and do what you are told. There is plenty of time for more of the story later."

Jimmy looked sad.

"Yes, ma'am." He went upstairs to change his clothes.

Scott didn't like reprimanding Jimmy and never wanted to overstep his bounds by correcting him when Barbara was there. He knew it wasn't easy raising a child on your own. Trying to teach him manners, respect, and right from wrong also wasn't easy when those things seemed to be a thing of the past. When did respect and manners become old-fashioned?

"Thank you," Barbara said.

"Nothing to thank me for," Scott said. "If he doesn't learn to respect you as a youngster, he never will as an adult."

Jimmy came back into the kitchen with a clean shirt, his favorite one, a Pennsylvania National Guard T-shirt. Scott had given it to him for his birthday last year.

"Did you put your dirty clothes in the hamper?" his mom asked.

"Yes," Jimmy answered. "If I didn't, Scott would make me go back upstairs and do it."

"You got that right," Scott said. "You have to help your mom as much as you can around the house."

"Can we go out and get something to eat?" Jimmy asked.

"I have a better idea," Barbara said. "Since Scott won't be here very long, how about I order a pizza, and you two can go and play video games downstairs."

"Really, Mom?" Jimmy said. "But it's a school night. I'm never allowed to play video games on a school night."

Barbara never let Jimmy play video games during the week. Monday through Thursday nights were for homework and studying. If she let Jimmy play when he got home from school, he would never get his homework or anything else done.

"This is a special occasion," she said. "Scott came a long way to see you. We can bend the rules this one time. We could move bedtime to nine thirty, as well."

"You're the best, Mom."

"I really wish I could have been at your school on Friday," Scott said. "I know how much you wanted me there. I really wanted to be there."

"It's okay," Jimmy said. "It would have been great if you could have been there. You would have liked all the stories from the other soldiers. And you could have met my teacher. She is really nice. She is the one who told me about the angels and how to make a wish into the universe. I can't wait to tell her you were waiting for me when I got home."

Scott still felt terrible about missing the big day at Jimmy's school. However, if Jimmy was okay with Scott being at his house even for a little while, he was okay with that.

Scott followed Jimmy downstairs. But he couldn't help but wonder about those angels. Could they be the same angels that had appeared in his dream? How was that possible? Yes, angels have wings, but did these angels use them to fly all over the place? This was all getting to be too much of a coincidence, but instead of overthinking this, he would put that aside, enjoy the time he had with Jimmy, and savor every bite of the pizza they were having for dinner.

Scott and Jimmy weren't the only ones headed downstairs. Bear followed them and made himself comfortable on one of his beds. He had many beds, one downstairs near the couch, one upstairs in the living room by the recliner, and one in Barbara's room by the foot of her bed.

Barbara was so happy they still lived in a town that had pizza delivery. It was real pizza from an authentic pizzeria, not like the franchise-owned places where you can get anything and everything as a topping. The owners of Nunzio's Pizzeria, Sal and Enzo Nunzio, were brothers. Their parents came to the United States in the 1960s from Abruzzo, Italy, a town east of Rome. They first moved to New York, but Sal had come to Pennsylvania to go to college and loved it, so in the early 1980s he moved his brother and parents to Harrisburg, and they opened up a pizza place. Everyone in Harrisburg was so grateful they did. They had the best pizza in the state.

The pizza arrived, and it smelled heavenly. It was a large pie, half sausage, half extra cheese. She didn't want to interrupt the boys playing their game, so she brought four slices of pizza down to them, two sausage and two cheese, so they could decide who would eat what. As soon as she opened the door to go downstairs, she heard the yelling.

"Dude, you made me hit the wall," Scott said.

"Move over or get run over," Jimmy answered him.

They were playing some kind of racing game. She wasn't even going to try and remember its name. There were too many games for her to remember all their names. She was amazed how Jimmy could remember every aspect of all those games but forget to put his lunch in his backpack almost every day.

She put the pizza and two bottles of iced tea on the table behind them and went back upstairs. There wasn't any reason to interrupt them, and they would smell the pizza and stop playing at some point. In the meantime, she would enjoy some quiet time to herself, something she rarely got.

Before she knew it, it was nine o'clock. The boys were coming upstairs carrying their plates and empty bottles. Jimmy needed to keep his bedtime. He was still young and needed his sleep. Scott needed to get ready to leave as well: 0600 comes early. He didn't want to be late getting to the base and miss the flight back to Afghanistan.

"Go get ready for bed, buddy," Scott said. "I'll put the dishes in the dishwasher for your mom."

Jimmy ran upstairs, changed into his pajamas, and brushed his teeth as fast as he could, so he could spend a little more time with Scott before he had to go to bed. Jimmy came downstairs in his camouflaged pajamas. It was time to say good night and goodbye to Scott.

"Are you sure you have to leave now?" Jimmy said. "Can't you stay a few more minutes?"

He didn't want his older brother to leave. No one knew when he was going to get his orders to come home for good.

"I'm sure, buddy," Scott said. "It's easier if I head back to the base. It's an early flight and a long one."

Jimmy ran over to Scott and hugged him.

"You be safe," Jimmy said. That was something that Scott always said. He never said goodbye. He always said to be safe. For Scott, goodbye was something he said at a fellow soldier's funeral because he would never see his brother-in-arms again. Telling people to be safe was not as final as goodbye in his mind.

"You bet," Scott said. "We have a rematch of that race when I come home. Don't you forget that. You be good for your mom. I'll be home before you know it."

Scott turned to Barbara and gave her a hug.

"You take care of yourself," she said. "See you when you get home. We will be at the base to welcome you home properly."

"Thank you," Scott said. "When I get home, I'll take Jimmy to my house for a weekend. You can go see your sister and plan a girls' trip. Go to a spa or do whatever you women do when you are together."

"I'm taking you up on that," Barbara said.

He had an hour before he had to check in at the base. He went to his house to look at it and maybe grab a quick shower before going back to the base to get some sleep. If he slept at home, he worried he wouldn't get up on time. It was easier to sleep at the base, so he could get on the never-ending flight back to Afghanistan.

Chapter 16
Somewhere over the Mediterranean

Scott made sure he was awake and on the tarmac by 0530. They were scheduled for takeoff at 0630, and he didn't want to keep anyone waiting. The flight crew had a schedule to keep, and he would make sure they stayed on it. One of his pet peeves was not being able to take off on time.

Captain David Boyd was already in the airplane, making sure all the cargo was accounted for and secured. The last thing a captain or a flight crew wanted was to hit turbulence and have crates full of supplies and equipment shift. Those crates contained weapons, ammunition, clothing, repair parts, and components for various vehicles and personal items. When soldiers were deployed for an extended period of time, they wanted silly things most people would take for granted, for instance, a Frisbee, a football, toothpaste, shaving cream, tea, hot chocolate, eye drops, sunscreen, even gummy bears. Captain Boyd—Pink—made sure the personal items were well secured. Although he was a soldier, he had the utmost respect for the men and women that were in theater. He didn't think that gummy bears would be classified as a personal item, but they were on the list, so he made sure they were on the plane.

Pink looked at this watch. It said 0600. They had half an hour before takeoff. He was getting ready for the preflight check

"Morning, Pink," Scott said.

"Hey, Scooter," Pink responded. "You're here early, and only pilots are early. I'm beginning to think you might be a pilot."

Pink was teasing Scott. Pilots always got to the airport earlier than they needed to. They had to check and double-check their aircraft before they took off.

"That I am, my friend. Anything I can do to help?"

"We are good to go," Pink said. "Just waiting on the rest of the crew. They went to get some coffee and whatever else they feel like eating."

"Roger that," Scott said. He found a place to sit and wait for the rest of the guys to show up.

Scott was waking up from a nap. He didn't realize he had fallen asleep. He was disoriented. It took him a second to get acclimated, with one hundred and fifty soldiers and cargo.

"Where exactly are we?" Scott asked one of the men.

"Somewhere over the Mediterranean," the man responded.

After sleeping for such a long time, Scott knew that he should get up and stretch his legs, but he didn't feel like it. Instead, he started thinking about Erika and the date he would take her on once his orders came in to be reassigned back home. Once they landed, he was going to send her an email and let her know he got back safely, just like he'd said he would. He wanted her to know he was a man who kept his word. That was very important to teach Jimmy. A real man keeps his word. Scott couldn't believe how much Jimmy had grown since Scott had been deployed. Jimmy was taller, more confident, and smarter, or maybe more of a smart aleck. That was it—definitely more of a smart aleck.

Scott loved flying planes, but he hated being a passenger, not having anything to do but sleep, read, and think. One thing nagging Scott was what Jimmy had said about the angels and how his teacher had told him to wish into the universe. Were his messenger and Jimmy's angel the same person? How could that be? Had she appeared to him in a dream, or was she really an angel that came to him? All these thoughts were racing through Scott's mind. He felt like a hamster on a wheel, thoughts going around in his head but not getting any logical answers. Maybe that was it. Maybe making a wish into the universe defied logic, and a person just had to have faith and trust that wishes come true.

Chapter 17
Watchtower Harbor
June 19

Today was the girls' last day of school. Just like all kids, Julia and Sophie thought that next to Christmas and their birthdays, the last day of school was the best day of the year. It was also a half day, which made it so much better. As the girls were on their way to school, the bickering started.

Julia loved to rub it in Sophie's face that she was the older sister. At times Julia did it just to get a reaction from Sophie, and it worked every time.

"I can't believe I am going into fourth grade," Julia said to her younger sister. "That means I will be a school safety monitor next year and boss you around."

"You always think you are the boss of me," Sophie said. "Well, you're not. Only Mommy and Daddy can tell me to do things."

"In school, I can boss you around," Julia said. "If you run in the hallways, I can tell you to stop, go back to the doors, and walk if I want to."

"If I see you in a hallway, I won't go down that way," Sophie said. "I will turn around and run down the other hallway that you aren't the boss of, so there."

Sophie was a feisty little girl. She was three years younger than Julia, but that didn't stop her from standing her ground. Younger sister or not, she was not going to be pushed around. As they approached the double door entrance, Julia reminded Sophie to meet her right there after school so that they could walk home together. Julia turned left to go to her classroom. Sophie stuck out her tongue and shook her head at her. If Julia didn't see it, Sophie wouldn't get into trouble.

Meanwhile, their mom, Annalise, was in the kitchen at the girls' home getting lunch ready because she knew they would be back soon. She had the radio on, louder than usual. She was listening to one of her all-time favorite songs, *Fantasy* by Earth, Wind & Fire. It reminded her of when she was little and her father would listen to his records while washing the cars or doing something in the yard. Whenever *Fantasy* was playing, her father would pick her up and dance around the garage or backyard. She carried on that tradition. When the girls were in school, and she was home doing things around the house, the radio was always on loud, and she would dance. Dancing made housework easier to do and time go by faster. As she made sure Julia had her yucky chips and Sophie had her barbeque chips on their plates, Annalise heard a delivery truck drive up to her street. She was hoping it was the boogie boards she had ordered for the girls. Originally, they were supposed to be delivered between the thirteenth and the sixteenth. But they were on backorder, so now they were supposed to come between the eighteenth and the twenty-first. Today being the nineteenth, she was hoping it was the boogie boards. She had also ordered things and forgotten what she ordered until she opened the box. She walked into the living room, looked out the window, and saw the UPS truck at the bottom of her driveway. It had to be the boogie boards. She was expecting her doorbell to ring. Joey, the UPS driver, rang whenever she had a delivery to let her know she had a package by the door. Several minutes passed, her doorbell didn't ring, and the UPS truck was still at the bottom of her driveway. She went outside to see if maybe it was a different driver, and he had left the package by the garage. As she was going down her front stairs, Joey walked up her driveway carrying a huge box. It was so bulky he probably should have used a hand truck and wheeled it up the driveway.

"Hi Joey," Annalise said. "That box is huge."

Now his delay in getting out of the truck made sense. He probably had to figure out how to carry that package.

"Hey, Annalise," Joey said. "It's a big box, but it's not heavy. What did you order?"

"Boogie boards for the girls."

"Boogie boards or surfboards?" Joey asked. "I have one more for you. Can you give me a hand? I have to move some boxes around to get to it."

"Sure."

As they walked to the truck, Joey asked her how her husband was doing. He knew her husband was a soldier and always asked about him. She appreciated that he cared enough to do that. They stopped as they got to the double doors at the back of the truck.

"If you can wait right here," he said, "I'll go in the truck and open up the double doors."

Joey went around the side of the truck and got in. Annalise heard him walking towards the back and unlock the doors. As he opened the doors, a huge box wasn't waiting for her, but her husband was.

She was so happy to see him. Her eyes were filled with tears of happiness. She hugged him tightly and didn't want to let him go. She hugged Joey and thanked him for delivering a wonderful surprise. Sean thanked him and shook his hand. Joey went back to work, and Sean and Annalise walked up the driveway.

"I was going to sneak into the house to surprise you," Sean said. "Then I saw the delivery truck and asked Joey if he was up to having a little fun, and he was all for it."

"It worked out really well," she said. "I would have never thought you would be hiding in a UPS truck."

She had missed him so much, and she hugged him again as they were walking towards the house.

"Where are the girls?" he asked as they released themselves from their long embrace.

It was a huge relief for her to have him back. He was home safe and sound, at least for now, until the next mission. However, she wasn't going to let that inevitable thought in her head. She was going to enjoy the feeling that he was home and how excited the girls would be to see him.

"They are in school, and today is their last day," Annalise said. "I can't wait to see them. Let's get them."

"Six months is way too long to be away from my girls."

"They have a half day today and should be home anytime."

Just as Annalise was finishing her sentence, the front door opened.

"Mom, we're home," Julia said. "Can we go to the beach?"

"That sounds like a fantastic idea," their father answered.

Chapter 18
Ralph Waldo Emerson Elementary School
June 25
Last Day of School

Every year on the last day of school, Ms Beck treated her class to an ice cream party. Ever since she was a little girl, ice cream had been her favorite dessert. If anyone asked her what her favorite food was, she would always respond by saying ice cream.

She couldn't say why ice cream was her favorite food when there were so many other types of food she loved and enjoyed eating. Maybe it was one of the many things she and her older brother had in common. Whenever he was home from wherever he was deployed and had errands to run, he would take her along, and they would end up at their favorite ice cream shop, Top This.

She loved the last day of school. For her, it wasn't about not working for the next two months. That was only true in theory. Come August, teachers were already busy thinking about their students, how they were going to set up their classroom, and how they were going to deal with a new group of parents who all thought their children shined brighter than the sun, when in fact, some of them were as bright as a flashlight. But Ms Beck wasn't going to have any of those thoughts right now. Right now, she didn't want to think about anything except chocolate syrup and sprinkles. The ice cream party was also her reward for working hard during the school year.

The three tables in the back where the kids had their reading groups during the school year were set up and ready to go. Ms Beck would be at the first table with a tub of vanilla and one of chocolate swirl. She scooped the ice cream into waffle bowls. This way, the kids only had to throw away their spoons because they would eat the bowls. She had been doing this a long time. She had learned that the more choices of flavors the kids had, the longer it took them to decide. If you gave them a choice between a cone or bowl, it would take them forever to decide about that, as well. For that reason, Ms Beck only bought waffle bowls; however, when they reached the toppings table, they had their choice of toppings.

Jimmy's mom was at the second table. Due to her work schedule, she didn't often get the chance to volunteer in the classroom. She had taken today off to join the other parents and have fun with Jimmy and his classmates. She was in charge of the chocolate syrup and the whipped cream. Table number three had all the different toppings: rainbow and chocolate sprinkles, mini chocolate chips, mini marshmallows, M&M's, gummy bears, gummy worms, chocolate chip cookies, and cherries.

"Boys and girls." Ms Beck was trying to get their attention and settle them down. "Once you are sitting at your desks quietly, with your hands folded, Mrs Andrews, Jimmy's mom, will point to the group that is the quietest, and you will come up first to get your ice cream."

Within seconds, all the kids had scrambled to their desks. The two women shook their heads. They couldn't believe how fast the kids had sat at their desks, folded their hands, and quieted down.

"Great job listening, boys and girls," Mrs Andrews said. "It's going to be tough choosing who will come up first."

"Why don't you use the popsicle sticks?" Emma called out.

"What are the popsicle sticks?" asked Mrs Andrews.

"They are sticks with all the kids' names on them," Ms Beck said. "It's a fair way of picking a student at random. It also keeps their attention because they have to be quiet so they can hear their name."

"What a great idea," Mrs Andrews said. "Thank you for that suggestion."

One by one, she pulled sticks out of the pink plastic cup. The ice cream had started melting, though, so she called out the names quickly. The kids came up to the tables and waited quietly for their turn. They got their ice cream, topped it with what they liked, and went back to their seats. The kids ate their ice cream and talked about all the fun things they would do that summer. They were quiet while waiting their turn but made a mess of all the toppings, so Mrs Andrews started cleaning the table.

The last day of school was a half day. Since Mrs Andrews was cleaning, Ms Beck had a chance to give the kids her last-day-of-school speech and get them ready for dismissal.

"One, two, three, all eyes on me." Ms Beck stood at the front of the classroom, waiting for the kids to look at her.

"First I want to say thank you for being a great class. Each of you has grown so much since last September. You started the school year only knowing how to add and subtract. Now all of you know how to multiply and divide. You can read chapter books on your own. You have accomplished so many great things. If you continue to believe in yourself and follow your dreams, you will achieve great things in your lives."

"And believe in angels," Jimmy shouted.

"And believe in angels," Ms Beck said, smiling at Jimmy and giving him a quick wink.

She was so happy she had shared her story and secret with Jimmy about making wishes from your heart. When you do, the universe heard them and made them come true.

Ms Beck realized she was talking too much. She told the kids to put their chairs on top of their desks.

"One last thing," she said. "Have a fantastic summer. I am going to miss all of you."

With that, the kids were dismissed, and the school year was over.

***

Watchtower Harbor
June 26

The girls had been out of school for a week. Since school ended, their days had been nonstop. Sean, the girls' father, was home safe from the latest mission which had seemed to last longer than previous ones. Then again, no one truly knew how long it would take for an assignment to be accomplished. It could be a couple of weeks, or it could last months.

Sean loved being a SEAL, but it wasn't an easy job, not for him, not for his wife, and not for their marriage or his family. It was meaningful and important work that made the world a safer place, though, and that was why he did it.

When Sean was home, his world revolved around his girls: Where they wanted to go, what they wanted to do, what they wanted to talk about. Today they didn't want to do much of anything. It was not a beach day. It had been raining all morning and was chilly for late June.

"Girls," their father called. "Is there anything you want to do today, maybe go somewhere?"

"Daddy," Sophie answered, "it's icky today. I think we should stay home and talk about the dollhouse you promised to build for me. Remember?"

"Of course I remember," he said. "I would never forget something as important as your dollhouse."

He really hadn't forgotten it. Thoughts of his family and doing things for his girls kept him going during the long days and nights when he was away from home.

"Yay!" Sophie cheered. "I want it to have three bedrooms, a living room, a staircase, and lights, so I can play at night. I'm going to tell Mommy right now. I'll be back."

"Can you make one for me too, Daddy?" Julia asked.

"Of course, darling," he answered.

Julia ran and hugged her father.

"Thank you, Daddy. I don't want one as big as Sophie's. I only want two bedrooms, but I want everything else her house will have."

Sean loved to see his girls happy. From the moment they were born, they'd had him wrapped around their fingers. His professional life was the polar opposite of his home life. On the one hand, he was as tough as nails, strong, stubborn, determined. On the other hand, he could be reduced to a puddle seeing his girls smile.

"Daddy," Julia said, "can I tell you about the little boy who had a wish and I helped him?"

"Of course, sweetheart."

Sean knew that his daughters were special and had a gift that allowed them to hear wishes other children sent out to the universe. It had started when Julia was five — years-old, and then for Sophie when she was four, and it was something they got from their mother. They headed over to the map on the wall, so she could point out to him where the little boy was from and where she had gone to make his wish come true.

"There was a little boy, and his name was Jimmy," Julia said. "He is eight like me, and lives in Harrisburg, Pennsylvania, which is over here, where the yellow pin is."

"I see the yellow pin," her father said.

"His older brother is in the Army, and Jimmy was missing him so much, just like the way we miss you when you are away, so I know how sad he was feeling."

A twinge of guilt hit Sean like a steam train. Of course his girls missed him, but hearing it brought a whole other level of heartache.

"His older brother is in Afghanistan. Remember when you were there, Daddy?"

"I remember," he said. "I was there last year. It was not a friendly country."

"I know, Daddy. I traveled there to give his older brother the message, to tell him to call Jimmy when he could, and he did."

"That's wonderful," Sean said. "You are a special little girl, but I already knew that."

"Oh, Daddy, you are so silly sometimes," she said.

Sean adored his little girls. He had always wanted to be a father. Once the girls were born, he had his family, and his life was complete.

"How about we talk about going on vacation?" he asked her.

"Sophie and I might want to stay home this summer," Julia said. "Some of our friends we met last year are coming back, and we want to play with them."

"I'm sure you will, honey," he said. "But I think we need a family vacation too, just like your friends have every year."

"Okay," she said. "How about Disney World or a cruise? One of my friends in school went on a cruise over the winter break. She said it was fun."

"Those are great ideas. Let's talk to Mom and Sophie about them and see what they say."

"Oh wait, Daddy. I just remembered my friend told me about the first night of the cruise, how she got sick at dinnertime and threw up all over her brother's shoes. Let's forget the cruise. If Sophie gets sick and throws up on my shoes, I'm going to be really mad at her. I'll dump my food over her head."

Sean couldn't help it. He started to laugh not because of what Julia had said but how fast she thought about what she would do.

"That settles that," he said. "We stay on land."

Chapter 19
Kandahar, Afghanistan
June 26

Scott had been back for a week. He was lying on his bunk, trying to catch up on his sleep. He and his team were waiting for the operations orders to come from the Pentagon, to see what the mission was going to be against the extremists. All his questions would be answered, including who, what, where, when, how, and why the operation was to be carried out.

What he really wanted were the orders to go home. Being home for two days had made him realize how homesick he was. For the first time since he joined the Army, he started to think a desk job wouldn't be a bad thing. Plus, Jimmy was growing up, and he needed a man in his life. He had an amazing mother, but she couldn't teach him things a boy needed to know, from the simple things like learning how to shave and how important a firm handshake is, to more confusing things like trying to understand girls, his first date, or his first broken heart, to being taught how important it is for a man to respect himself, his mother, and in the future, his wife.

Then there was Erika, the general's daughter he had met at the Pentagon. He did his best to maintain his composure, keep his eye on the objective, and stay focused. But this girl had thrown him for a loop. He had emailed her twice so far since he got back, and she had answered him, giving him hope that the dinner date he had promised her when he got home might happen.

His brain was racing. He needed to shake all those thoughts loose and clear his head. He jumped up, got off his bunk, and decided to go and do a safety check on the helicopters. They had to be ready to go at a moment's notice. It would keep his mind busy, and maybe he would stop thinking about going home. He didn't believe that, but he was going to try.

An hour later, Mike called Scott and his team into the office. The orders had come in from the Pentagon. Scott didn't feel like sitting in a meeting and dealing with all the military protocol about the upcoming mission. Nevertheless, he had to sit through the meeting and listen to what was said.

Mission: Code name Eagle Eye

Objective: Blow up the weapons cache stored in the warehouse.

Communication: There would be radio silence.

When: 28 June at 0300.

The last thing that Mike said caught Scott's attention more than anything else.

"Gentlemen," Mike said. "If this mission is a success, the next orders we receive will be to go home. Make it a successful one. Failure is not an option."

"Failure is never an option," Scott said as he headed out the door. He might not have been one hundred percent sure of himself in his personal life, but he was more than one hundred percent sure of himself and his team when it came to any mission. And after this mission was done, he was one hundred and ten percent sure he wanted to go home.

28 June 0000

Scott and his team were all suited up and ready to go. They knew it would take time to get to the warehouse where the weapons were being stored.

The last of the safety checks were being done, and it was almost time to tango, which meant time to head over to where the enemy, or at least their warehouse, was, and say goodbye to it once and for all. It might still be June, but when the warehouse hit the sky, it would light up like the Fourth of July!

The only sounds were the click-click-click of the switches, the whistling of the rotors, and the whump, whump, whump of the propellers as they beat the air into submission.

The men were just about to take off when Mike's voice came over their headsets. They had not gone into radio silence yet, so they could hear him loud and clear. No one could believe what he was saying.

"Gentlemen," Mike said. "Stand down. The mission has been scrapped."

"Excuse me?" Scott said. "Say again."

"The mission has just been scrapped. Shut everything down and meet me in my office ASAP."

The men on Scott's team were confused. Scott was infuriated. You can't just scrap a mission, he thought. After all the preparation and the time it had taken to get the plan together, not to mention get himself and his crew in the right frame of mind, there had better be a good reason for this colossal screw-up. For Scott and his men, getting ready psychologically was as important as the safety checks on the helicopters.

By the time he got to Mike's office, Scott was fit to be tied. He pushed the door so hard it almost came off the hinges. Mike looked at Scott the way a father would look at his son if he were being disrespected.

"You want to go outside and try coming back in again nicely?" Mike said. "I'm still your commanding officer, and you will show some respect. I don't care how mad you are."

"I'm so sorry, sir," Scott said. "All the time that was put into planning this, all the back and forth scouting missions can't be for nothing. Mike, although I am thankful you made it possible for me to see Jimmy, I flew to Washington for this mission, and now it's scrapped, for the love of God. None of this makes sense."

"That's enough, sergeant," Mike said. "I know you're annoyed, but don't take it out on me. I wasn't happy when I was told the mission was scrapped, either, but there is a good reason."

Mike had known Scott long enough to know the adrenaline was affecting Scott's mood. However, that didn't excuse Scott's behavior.

"There is always a good reason. I can't wait to hear it. Did the enemy declare a ceasefire at the last minute or—"

"I said that's enough," Mike cut Scott off mid-sentence. "If you can keep your mouth shut for half a second, I will tell you."

Scott didn't say another word.

"The reason why the mission was scrapped was that the warehouse and the weapons in it were destroyed within the last twelve hours. I don't know all the facts, but it seemed someone got to them before we did."

"Who?" Scott said.

"Did you not just hear what I said? I don't have all the facts. But I do know that unless they have another mission for us, we are heading home very soon. Now get some sleep. We will talk more about this when I know more. Dismissed."

.

Chapter 20
Later that same night

Scott had done his best to get some sleep, but too many things were racing through his mind, first of all what Mike had said. The mission had been scrapped because the warehouse had been destroyed. Had the British military hit the warehouse? But that didn't make sense. Scott had been working closely with the British. When you were working with another country, you knew what that country's plans were. Chances were it wasn't the Brits. Maybe it was a different force, but if so, who?

Scott was not a violent person and hated fighting of any kind. Despite being a soldier, he was quiet, almost bashful. He believed in fairness. He would just have to wait and see what Mike found out.

What kept him from sleeping was the way he had spoken to Mike with such frustration and disrespect. He and Mike had been good friends for years and had a long history. When Scott's father died, Mike had been there for him, helping him through his grief and giving him advice about how to help Jimmy cope with losing his dad at such a young age.

The more Scott thought about his behavior, the more he shrunk from embarrassment. He went from five-nine to the size of a garden gnome, and he was looking for a mushroom to hide under. First thing in the morning, he would apologize to Mike, maybe bring him a jelly doughnut as a peace offering.

Then there was Erika. This girl was driving him crazy. He'd had girlfriends in the past and platonic friends that were girls. But there was something special about Erika. He had promised to take her out to dinner when he got home. That raised more questions. Where would they go? Hershey Park? The Smithsonian Institute? What kind of flowers should he buy her? Roses? Carnations? An orchid? No, not an orchid. He wasn't taking her to prom. Scott was becoming slaphappy. The sun was going to come up soon, and if he didn't get to sleep, he wasn't going to be able to function. Maybe if he counted sheep, that would help. But he was in the Middle East. Perhaps he should count camels? With that, he drifted off.

He woke up at 0900, got dressed, and went over to the mess hall for some coffee. A few doughnuts were left, and he knew how much Mike loved doughnuts, especially powdered raspberry. One raspberry was left. He took it and headed over to Mike's office. It was a perfect way to break the ice and apologize.

"Hey, Badger," Scott said. "Is Mike in his office?" Scott loved Badger's nickname. It fit him to a tee. Nice enough guy, Scott thought, but the biggest pain in the neck in the Army.

"Yes, he's in there," Badger replied. "I have earplugs on my desk in case you feel like yelling at him again."

After his behavior yesterday, Scott deserved that dig. Still, he didn't want to hear it.

"You're not funny," Scott said. "You know what would be funny, corporal, you doing push-ups in the mess hall while everyone was eating lunch and you singing 'On Top of Spaghetti.' That would be funny."

Badger turned around and starting moving papers around his desk as if he were looking for something important. He wanted Scott to go away.

Scott knocked on Mike's door.

"Come in," Mike said. "Oh, Scooter, it's you. Thought you would try a more civil approach this time?"

"That's why I'm here with doughnuts, as a peace offering. I apologize; I don't know why I acted like that. I feel horrible. The only reason I can come up with is that I had too much adrenaline. When the mission was scrapped at the last second, my emotions got the better of me. I know better, and you are the last person I would ever disrespect. All I can say is I'm sorry. "

"Scott," Mike answered, "you don't think I know you better than that? I know exactly how you get before a mission. That's why I wanted you on my team and a part of my squadron so many years ago. You're committed, and you give everything you've got to make sure the mission is completed and your guys come back safely. You're one of the most professional and respectful guys in the military. But you lost your cool and yelled at a commanding officer. You know better than that."

"Yes, I do. It won't happen again."

"You got that right. If it does, you will be the one doing push-ups in the mess hall. Now give me my doughnut."

Scott felt better. He had apologized, and everything was going to be okay between them.

"Any word on what happened last night?" Scott asked. "Did the Brits get them?"

"Nope," Mike said.

"No? Then who did?"

"It turns out there was a rogue militant within their group."

This conversation wasn't making any sense to Scott. Generally, an extremist soldier would never double-cross his group. He knew his place was within the group and what was expected of him. Furthermore, they all worked towards the same goal, world domination. Like any organization, terrorist groups had a pecking order. A subordinate would never try to overtake a higher-ranking person. It showed a complete lack of respect, and it simply was not done.

"Wait," Scott said. "Someone in their group went rogue, or did they trust someone they shouldn't have?"

Mike was tapping his finger on his nose.

"You got it," Mike said. "They were double-crossed by someone they trusted."

"So, was the warehouse destroyed as well?" Scott said.

"No," Mike said. "The rogue militant and his organization just cleared it out and left the building untouched."

"Are you kidding me?" Scott said.

"This intel came from a very reliable source. I couldn't be more serious," Mike said. "The old saying is true. Be careful who you trust because salt and sugar look the same."

"Roger that," Scott said.

Chapter 21
Kandahar, Afghanistan

It was July in Afghanistan. During the day, the heat was oppressive. The moment Scott walked outside, a wall of heat hit him in the face. If the men of Strategic Air Command had their choice, no one would leave their air-conditioned tents until after the sun went down. Unfortunately, they didn't have a choice because there was work to be done. Even though a rogue extremist had done their job for them the other night, the helicopters still had to be ready, which meant maintenance, maintenance, and more maintenance. Scott headed over to the landing area where the helicopters were. He was a stickler for detail. He would never go up in any aircraft unless he was sure it was 100 percent ready to go. Being the lead pilot and senior member of his crew, he would never send his crew up in a helicopter that he hadn't checked and double-checked.

He couldn't believe the heat. It would have been 125 degrees in the shade if there were shade to be found. But no trees were around, just sand as far as the eye could see. It was so hot that Scott was waiting for the sand to turn into glass.

He and Kevin, one of the helicopter's maintenance guys, worked on the gearbox and the tail rotor, inspecting the flanges that acted as connectors between the tail rotor and the power drive. Most pilots knew about the aircraft they were flying but didn't want to have to repair them.

Scott had always wanted to be in the mix, learning not just how to fly helicopters but also how to repair them if he had to. The last thing Scott would want on a mission was to have a malfunction he did not know how to repair, putting himself and his co-pilot in danger.

It had to be the hottest day in history as far as Scott was concerned.

He looked up in the sky, hoping clouds would cover the sun even for a few minutes—no such luck. The sky was a brilliant light blue as far as his eyes could see. "You know," Scott said, "when I was a kid, my grandfather would always say, 'It's so hot you can fry an egg on the sidewalk'. Today I think if we had a sidewalk, we would be able to cook a steak."

"You got that right," Kevin agreed. "If we had some corn on the cob, it would turn into popcorn before we had the chance to shuck it."

"The heat finally got to you," Scott said, shaking his head. "That wasn't even funny. It was just wrong."

"Then why are you laughing?"

"The heat got to me too," Scott said.

He went to the cooler and grabbed two bottles of water. He threw one to Kevin.

"That's to pour over your head for saying such a bad joke," Scott said. "Let's get back to work."

Kevin finished up working on the gearbox with Scott's help. It took an hour. He finished putting his tools away, closed both his toolboxes, and asked Scott if he could grab the gearbox because his hands were full. Scott was daydreaming, a million miles away.

"Sarge," Kevin said.

No reply from Scott, so Kevin called out to him again.

"Sarge. Holy cow, whoever she is, she must be something. You completely zoned out. Let's go get some chow."

Scott wasn't going to respond to anything Kevin had just said about daydreaming or zoning out. His private life was just that—private—but Kevin was right. Erika was something. Scott was daydreaming about her, making plans for when he got home, taking her out to dinner, going to the movies. If she liked amusement parks, he would take her to Hershey Park for sure.

"Lunchtime already?" Scott asked. "Time flew by this morning."

"You can change the subject all you want, sarge. But you can't change your face from turning beet-red. I assure you, that's not sunburn."

***

While everyone was eating, Mike went into the mess hall. Generally, Badger got Mike's lunch for him, but today Mike had an announcement and wanted to do it in person rather than over the loudspeaker.

"Attention," Badger called out. Everyone stood up.

"Carry on," Mike said. He wanted them to continue eating. No need for them to stop. Once he told them what he had to say, they weren't going to finish, anyway. He asked Badger to announce that they should all stay once they finished eating.

"May I have everyone's attention for a minute," Badger said. "The colonel has an announcement he has to make and would like everyone to stay put once they have finished with chow."

The tent was silent. It reminded Scott of church when he was a kid, when the priest walked up to the altar and within a nanosecond the whole congregation stopped talking. It made sense that the tent went silent because no one knew how to take what Badger had just said. The scuttlebutt was that they were going home. But if that were it, wouldn't Mike just come out and say it? Then again, maybe he wouldn't.

Mike got a cup of coffee and a doughnut and sat down with Scott and his flight crew. All the men at the table were talking about what they would do once they got home. One of them was Peter Burton, the flight engineer, whose wife had had a baby two months ago. He was talking about how bad he felt missing the birth of his daughter. He was hoping to get home before she took her first steps. It happens to many soldiers. They miss important milestones in their children's lives. Unfortunately, that is the nature of the beast. Peter knew he was luckier than the men who would never see any milestones in their children's lives.

Mike looked around the mess hall. Everyone seemed to be done with lunch. He stood and made his way to the center of the tent. Everyone looked at him.

"Gentlemen," Mike started. "We have been in Afghanistan for nine months. We have missed holidays, birthdays, and anniversaries with our families. For some of you, this has been your first tour. Others have been here two or three times. The Pentagon thanks you, I thank you, and the people of the United States of America are grateful for your service. It's been my honor and privilege to stand beside you and fight for what we believe in.

"I have been in communications with the Pentagon. I got off the phone with General Pierce an hour ago. Our replacements will be here the fifteenth of this month. Pack your bags. We are going home."

The tent erupted in cheers, handshakes, and hugs. Those words were music to the men's ears. Mike wasn't going to formally dismiss them after his announcement. He just let them enjoy the moment. He returned to the table where Scott and his crew were. Scott was the first person at the table to shake Mike's hand and thanked him for being a good commander and making sure they didn't have to extend their tour.

"One last thing, gentlemen," Mike said to Badger, Kevin, and Scooter, who were sitting at the table. "Once we get home, and all of us have spent time with our families, Watchtower Harbor, one of my favorite vacation spots when my kids were younger, has its bicentennial celebration. My wife has rented a huge place. It has three cottages, in addition to the main house. "I'll never be able to retire if I don't curb her spending. Anyway, we would like the three of you and your families to join us that weekend. Once we get home, I'll touch base with you. Scooter, make sure you bring Jimmy and that pretty general's daughter you have been emailing."

Scott looked surprised. He hadn't told Mike anything, not yet, anyway. So how could he know about Erika?

"Next time, Sergeant Andrews," Mike continued, "when you use the computer in my office, close all the tabs when you are finished. Start gathering up your gear. The fifteenth isn't that far away. We will talk later."

The other two men left to go to their tents and start packing. They weren't going to wait for the last minute to get their things together.

"Oh no we won't," Scott said. He was turning red and looking down at the table, hoping to regain his composure before he said anything else.

"Oh yes we will," Mike responded. "Inquiring minds want to know."

With that, Scott left the mess hall, knowing that once he got back to his tent, his flying partner and good friend would also want to know everything about the general's pretty daughter.

Chapter 22
Harrisburg, Pennsylvania
Ralph Waldo Emerson Elementary School
Mid-August

Towards the end of August, teachers had to start reporting to school to set up their classrooms, attend meetings, and get ready for the new school year. Like most teachers, Ms Beck was filled with both excitement and dread as she stood in the middle of her classroom. She was excited for the new school year to start, but she had a lot of work ahead of her. First, she needed to set up her new classroom. At the end of the last school year, which was only two months ago, she had packed up her old classroom and moved it to another part of the school, down the hallway from where her old classroom was. This year she thought it would be a good idea to go to school a week early to get ready, so she wasn't scrambling at the last minute to get everything done. Besides, if she needed help from one of the custodians, they would have more time. It would help if she brought a box of doughnuts or a tray of sandwiches from the supermarket for them. Custodians did a lot of essential work at the school, so showing them a little appreciation went a long way.

  She didn't want to think about all the work she had to do. She would look on the bright side, concentrate on her new students. This year, according to her roster, she had more girls than boys, which meant the classroom was going to be chatty and filled with drama. With girls came drama about everything. With boys, the classroom was filled with talk about what level they were on in the latest video game. They talked about sports and bragged to each other about what exotic sports car they would have once they were old enough to drive. Little did the boys realize that any kind of car they would own when they finally got their driver's license would come with a big insurance premium and lots of rules of the road. For now, let them dream. When Ms Beck was eight, she had dreamed about living in Barbie's Dream House. Who wouldn't want to live in a house with three floors and an elevator? When she grew up and realized she would have to clean all three floors, she changed her mind about having a big house, with or without an elevator.

She had better get started opening the boxes and see what was in them. Her students last year had helped her pack up the classroom but didn't label the boxes even after she reminded them ten times. Chances were she would set up this classroom to look just like her old classroom. She didn't have to try and remember where things were because everything would be in the same place as it was last year. She liked to keep things simple. She had the radio on and was singing while she was unpacking the boxes. She kept the volume down just in case another teacher or custodian walked into her room to say hi. Then one of her and Matt's favorite songs, *Come Sail Away* by Styx, came on, and she turned the volume from two to eight.

She started dancing while she was emptying boxes. One song had totally changed her energy level. While she didn't care who saw her, she was also thankful that no one walked in while she was singing and dancing. Her phone was vibrating and moving across her desk. When she picked it up, she had a missed call and voicemail message from Matt. She was happy to see he had called. She pushed the buttons to access her voicemail.

"Mops, it's Matt. We are thinking about going away the last week in August, and I want you to come with us. Call me when you get a chance."

She called him right back.

"Hi Mops," Matt said. "How are you?"

"I'm doing well," she said. "I'm in my new classroom setting it up for the school year."

"Already?" Matt asked. "When does school start?"

"After Labor Day. But I wanted to get a jump on things, set up my classroom and get that out of the way."

"You are the most dedicated teacher I've ever met," Matt told her. "Are you going to do the project with the veterans again this year? That was a lot of fun."

"I think I am," Jessica said. "It was a lot of work. I may not wait until June, but I think I will do it. The kids learned and had a lot of fun."

"Am I invited again this year, or was it just a one-time deal?"

"I have to think about it. You were the most boring one there. I think one of the teachers fell asleep while you were talking."

"Ha, ha, ha. Aren't you funny?"

"As a matter of fact, I am."

They loved to tease each other, just like most siblings did. It was light-hearted banter. They loved doing that with each other.

"Tell me about where you are going," Jessica said. "I want to go with you. I didn't go anywhere exciting this summer. I want to go somewhere before school starts."

"I was thinking about going to Watchtower Harbor," he said. "We haven't been there since we were kids. They are having their bicentennial celebration. I think it would be fun for all of us to go."

"Watchtower Harbor?" she said. "Holy cow, I love Watchtower Harbor. We haven't been there in forever. Absolutely! It will be just like we were kids again, when we went with Mom and Dad. You know, Matt, I think Mom and Dad would love the idea that we are going back to a place where we had so much fun with them when we were kids."

"I think so, too," he said.

"Now I really have to finish up my room," Jessica said.

She wanted to change the subject and not talk about their parents, who had passed away within six months of each other. Their mother had passed away from bone cancer. Six months later, Jessica's father had died, and she was convinced it was from a broken heart from missing his wife. It had been eight years, but talking about them still made her very sad.

"Okay," Matt said.

Chapter 23
Kandahar, Afghanistan

Two days. Forty-eight short hours and we will be home, Scott thought as he was lying on his bunk. All morning, he had been working closely with the new flight crew that was replacing his crew. He had been going over the maintenance records for the helicopters, briefing the new guys on where the extremists were and where he thought they might be setting up new terrorist cells. Scott tried desperately to keep things in proper perspective and not get excited about going home, but it was difficult because he couldn't get Erika off his mind. He and his men had been in the desert way too long, dealing with scorching temperatures, the sun, sandstorms, and bugs.

Not even pretty bugs, either, like butterflies or ladybugs or even lunar moths. Nope, the desert had giant black scorpions that had to be at least four inches long. The first time Scott saw a scorpion was on his pillow. He thought one of his men was playing a trick on him. It was so big and scary-looking he thought it was plastic, the kind they sell as a gag gift in the Dollar Store. Then it started moving. It was no joke. The only thing he hated more than bugs were needles. Somehow he had to find the guts to get this horrible-looking thing off his pillow without screaming like a little girl. He ended up picking up his pillow by the corners and flinging the scorpion across his tent. He didn't even care where it landed.

He wouldn't miss the camel spider, either. They were the ugliest things he had ever seen and had to be the size of his hand. They were the color of sand, so you couldn't see them until they were crawling on you. Scott wasn't going to miss those. The more he thought about going home and leaving those bugs behind, the happier he became. He was happy he was going to see Jimmy and Barbara, this time for good. He decided he was going to apply for a desk job. Six months ago, he would have balked at the idea of sitting behind a desk for the rest of his career. However, life has a way of changing a person's thinking.

Jimmy was getting older and needed a father figure. Not that Scott knew much about being a father, but he would do his best. He could at least teach Jimmy how to be a man of integrity and be responsible. Scott could teach Jimmy the importance of keeping his word, being a gentleman at all times, and respecting women as well as himself. Scott could teach Jimmy the importance of a firm handshake and looking people in the eye when he was speaking to them. Then, when Jimmy was old enough, teach him how to shave and drive.

Erika was the other reason Scott was putting in for a desk job. He wanted to spend some time with her and get to know her better. He wasn't sure how it was all going to play out. He lived in Harrisburg, and she lived in Virginia, but for now, he wasn't going to worry about that. He didn't want to overthink things. He was just going to wait and see what happened and take it one day at a time.

He was making himself nuts thinking of too many things, like what Jimmy needed, Scott's next career move, Erika, what time the transport plane would be there tomorrow, and their flight home the day after that. He was giving himself a headache. He left his tent and went to the mess hall to grab a cup of coffee, thinking he would head over to Mike's office to see what he was up to.

As luck would have it, Mike walked out of the mess hall as Scott was walking in.

"I was going to grab some coffee," Scott said, "then head over to your office."

"Let me guess," Mike said, "you need to use my computer to talk to your girlfriend."

"I don't need your computer, and she isn't my girlfriend."

"Just a matter of time," Mike said.

Scott got his coffee, grabbed a raspberry cheese pastry, and headed to Mike's office. It didn't bother him that Mike was teasing him about Erika. They had been friends for ten years. It was all in good fun. Mike was the closest thing to an older brother Scott would ever have. Scott knew if he would ever get married, he would ask Mike to be his best man.

Strangely enough, Badger wasn't in Mike's office. Mike's door was open.

"Where is your sidekick?" asked Scott.

"His sister just had a baby," Mike said. "He went to call or Skype or whatever this generation does."

Mike wasn't a fan of all the different ways of communicating. He hated his cell phone. He called it a tracking device. He didn't like that he could be found any place on earth. He enjoyed being alone and not interrupted by his phone ringing or someone texting him. Why would people text him, anyway? He told everyone if you text me, I'm not responding. You want something, call me. He was fifty-two, so he wasn't old, just old-school.

Scott sat, put his coffee on Mike's desk, and started to eat his Danish.

"Looking forward to heading home?" Mike asked. "Seeing Jimmy and the general's daughter?"

"It's finally settling into my brain," Scott said, "that we are going home, so to answer your question, yes. I am."

"Good. We've been here way too long."

"Roger that," Scott said.

"Since you're here," Mike said. "Let me give you the details of the bicentennial celebration."

Mike gave Scott all the information he would need. He gave him the address of the house and also said Scott was responsible for barbequing the spare ribs he always boasted about.

"You know," Scott said, "this could have waited until we got home."

"You're probably right," Mike answered. "But I'm you giving all the information now. Who knows how much time I will have when I get home or what my wife has planned?"

Scott started to laugh. He loved Mike's wife. She was always nice to him and made the best chili he'd ever had.

He also knew how over-the-top she could be. No doubt she was planning something for Mike's homecoming.

"You talk to your girlfriend lately?" Mike asked.

"Does she know you are going home?"

"She knows," Scott said. "In case you are wondering, I am not going to see her as soon as I get home."

"You're not?" Mike said. "Why not? Is there something wrong with you?"

"No, nothing is wrong—"

"Then what is your problem?" Mike cut Scott off mid-sentence.

"If you would let me finish," Scott replied. "She won't be home until the twentieth. Her best friend from college is getting married in Colorado."

"Oh, okay," Mike said. "That makes sense."

Scott finished his coffee. He threw his cup and napkin in the trash. He told Mike he would see him later and headed out the door.

August 15

The day finally came to go home. Scott and his crew loaded their gear and bags along with other equipment and components that needed repairing but couldn't be fixed at the base onto the transport plane. They were headed back to Harrisburg.

The men were making noise and celebrating as they loaded everything up. You might have thought they were kids, and it was the last day of school. Who could blame them? Some of the men hadn't seen their families in over a year.

As the last box was loaded into the plane and the doors were locked, Mike once again thanked his men for the outstanding job they had done and for their dedication to making the world a safer place. Before they sat down and strapped in for the long flight, each one of them shook Mike's hand and thanked him for his support and his leadership.

As the plane taxied down the runway, the reality of going home set in. Scott couldn't wait. He could sleep in his bed, eat good food, and sit on his back deck looking at the maple and oak trees in his yard, enjoying the wind through their leaves and hearing the cardinals sing as they landed on his bird feeders and ate the seeds he would put out for them once he got settled in. Scott hadn't told Jimmy or Barbara he was coming back. Barbara had mentioned in an email that Jimmy would be going to camp for a couple weeks that summer, but as luck would have it, a couple of days after Scott got home Jimmy would be home from camp as well. Scott wanted to see the look of surprise on Jimmy's face when he saw his big brother.

Scott wanted to take Erika to Watchtower Harbor. Was it too soon to ask her to go away with him? They had only met face to face that one time at the Pentagon but kept in touch over email. Did that make her more of a pen pal or an "e-pal" instead of a girlfriend? Suppose after he got home, she didn't want to see him because a soldier lost his charm when he was no longer deployed? What would happen if she didn't like Jimmy or Jimmy didn't like her? Once again, he was playing twenty questions, overthinking things. It would be a good idea to go to sleep and not wake up until he was on American soil, or else he would drive himself nuts.

Chapter 24
Watchtower Harbor

For the first time in a long time, Sean was going to be home alone. Annalise, Connie, and the girls were leaving for the day. They were going shopping for a wedding dress. Connie, Annalise's younger sister, had gotten engaged in July while she and her boyfriend—now fiancé—were on vacation in the Bahamas. Sean liked Connie's fiancé, Rick. He was a nice guy for the most part, but on the quiet side. He was a high school history teacher. They came from two different worlds. If Sean had to live his life over again, maybe he would be a school teacher. Work five days a week, every holiday off, two months' vacation every summer—it sounded great. But maybe it was only nice in theory. Sean would never have the patience to be confined to a classroom day after day, year after year.

 The girls were ready. They couldn't wait to go wedding dress shopping. They were excited because Connie had asked if they would like to be her flower girls, and of course they said yes. If they had time, they would look for flower girl dresses, too. Annalise was going to be the matron of honor. Sean hadn't been asked to be one of Rick's groomsmen. Not yet, anyway. Generally, men didn't ask their friends to be groomsmen eighteen months before the wedding.

"Bye, Daddy," the girls yelled as they ran out the door to their Aunt Connie's car.

"Bye, sweethearts," Sean answered them. "Have a good time."

Annalise hugged him and said goodbye.

"I'm not sure what time we will be back," she said. "You know how my sister is. It takes her an hour to decide what size box of Band-Aids she should get."

Sean laughed because it was true. Connie had to be the most indecisive person on the planet.

"Don't worry about it," Sean said. "You had better get going before your sister starts beeping the horn."

"See you later, hon." Annalise walked out the door.

Sean went out back, sat on one of the lounge chairs under the big oak, and lit a cigarette. He tried not to smoke when he was home from a mission. He smoked enough when he was deployed. It calmed his nerves, so he could think clearly about the next moves his team needed to make. He never smoked around the girls or in the house. But now, he wasn't thinking about what he was doing. When he was deep in thought, lighting a cigarette was second nature for him.

He was still thinking about leaving his team for a desk job. His girls had grown up so fast. He'd already missed a big part of their childhood. He hated that. He wondered how much more he would miss because of the extremists, drug lords, pirates, and all the other deranged and demented people running loose in the world. On the other hand, his girls and all the other children in the world were exactly why he was doing what he was doing. He wanted them to grow up happy, safe, and free from danger.

Before he became a father, when he and Annalise were dating, Sean had been in the Navy for five years but wasn't yet a SEAL. Annalise was a paralegal working for a law firm that specialized in real estate. They were twenty-three, in love, no worries, no responsibilities, not a care in the world. They only knew that they wanted to get married, travel, and start a big family with at least six kids. But as much as Annalise wanted to be a mom, six was too many kids for her. She'd suggested a compromise, maybe three kids, a dog, and a cat. The memory made him smile.

Time to mow the lawn and trim the hedges. If Sean didn't get up and start moving, he would spend the rest of the day sleeping under the tree.

Chapter 25
Harrisburg, Pennsylvania
Air National Guard Base

"Touchdown!" Scott said to himself. After fourteen hours and twelve minutes, he was home. Even though he had been here a couple of months ago, that had been part of a mission, and he'd known he was flying back to Afghanistan. Everything had gone wrong on that trip except for getting to see Jimmy and Barbara and meeting Erika. He had also met Captain David "Pink" Boyd and his crew. Now, Captain Boyd was the pilot bringing Scott home.

The plane finished taxiing and came to a stop, giving everyone a jolt. Pink's voice came over the intercom.

"Gentlemen," Pink said, "allow me to be the first person to say welcome home and job well done. You made the base, the citizens of Harrisburg, and the United States proud by your service and your dedication. Glad you made it back safely."

The plane erupted with cheers, loud clapping, and ear-splitting whistling. All of the soldiers were happy to be home, see their loved ones, sleep in their beds, and eat home-cooked meals. Being stationed in the Middle East, certain things were off-limits, like eating pork and drinking alcohol. After nine months, the men missed having those things. One of them sitting towards the back of the plane shouted that tomorrow, he would have bacon and eggs for breakfast, a BLT for lunch, and a bacon-wrapped steak with a cold beer for dinner. Everyone burst out laughing, probably because they were thinking the same thing. Scott knew who was shouting. It was Donny Checkit, one of the flight engineers for the other team that flew day missions. In Scott's mind, Donny was one of the best. Scott was laughing along with the rest of them. That boy loved bacon more than he did his wife.

One by one, they shook the flight crew's hands and thanked them for a safe flight. All of them were anxious to grab their gear and go home, but they couldn't, not yet. First, they had to head into one of the airplane hangars to be officially dismissed by their commander. Scott stayed back and talked to Pink for a few minutes. No one was waiting for him. He hadn't told anyone he was coming home. That was the way he wanted it. He didn't like fanfare. Of course, he understood people missing their loved ones. But to be a soldier meant you could be away from your family for a long time. That was the nature of the beast. People knew it when they enlisted. Scott had told Mike he would help Pink and his crew go over the checklist and unload the plane. Scott would report to the commander when he was done.

As Pink and Scott were reading the gauges and going over the flight instruments, they started talking.

"Don't you want to go home and be with your family?" Pink asked.

"Absolutely," Scott said. "But it's just my younger brother and his mother, and he is away at camp for another two days. I will surprise them both when he comes home."

"Roger that," Pink said.

After Mike dismissed the men, he went back to the plane to get Scott.

"Hey Scooter, I'll drive you home," Mike said. "I signed out a car. Gail had to rush to the emergency room. Her mother was mopping the floors and slipped. I'm not sure if she broke anything."

Gail was Mike's wife. She had never missed one of Mike's homecomings. But this time, it couldn't be helped.

"Sounds like a plan," Scott said. "Let me check in with the commander first. Then I'll be ready to go."

"I already took care of that," Mike said. "You're good."

Scott shook Pink's hand, thanking him for a safe trip. They made plans to go out one night, soon.

The twenty-minute ride to Scott's house was quiet. They were both exhausted from the fourteen-hour flight, and Mike was worried about his mother-in-law. Scott had met Gail's mother a few times. She was a nice lady and an excellent cook. That's where Gail got it from. He was hoping that she hadn't broken anything.

On the way to Scott's house, Mike stopped at the mini-mart. Scott's refrigerator was probably empty, and he might need some milk for his coffee tomorrow.

"I thought you might want to pick up a few things before I dropped you off," Mike said.

"Always watching out for me," Scott said. "I know you want to get home, too. I could have walked to the store once I got back."

Both men headed into the store. Mike wanted to get a bottle of A&W. It was his favorite. Scott teased him about drinking root beer. He would tell Mike that he would be able to drink real beer with the big boys one day, but for now, he should stick to what he could handle, root beer.

Scott picked up a quart of milk, a box of Frosted Flakes, and a pre-packaged ham sandwich that had a sticker on it that said "freshly made daily." Scott didn't care when it was made. He just knew he was hungry. He grabbed a bag of barbeque potato chips to go with the sandwich and a bottle of Dr Pepper. That should hold him over until tomorrow, when he could go grocery shopping and stock up his pantry.

After they pulled into Scott's driveway, Mike opened his trunk so Scott could get his duffle bag with his gear and clothes. He grabbed the shopping bag as well. He went over to the driver's side to say goodbye to Mike and thank him for the ride.

"Keep me posted on Gail's mom," Scott said. "If you or Gail need anything, I'm a phone call away."

"Thanks," Mike said. "She is a tough old bird. She will be fine."

"Roger that," Scott answered.

"I'll call you in a few days, when I find out what the final plans are for a getaway in Watchtower Harbor."

"Okay," Scott said. "I'll be around."

By the time Scott reached the top step of his house, Mike had pulled out of his driveway and disappeared down the road.

Scott was so glad he had installed a keyless entry on his front door. He hated to fumble with keys when his hands were full. The code was easy enough to remember—Jimmy's birthday 9-2-3.

It was almost surreal being home. After being away for close to a year, Scott had to get used to the quiet and serenity of sitting on his couch, watching TV, and sleeping in a real bed. He was grateful to Barbara for keeping an eye on his house and airing it out. He hated the way a house smelled when it had been closed up for a long time.

In the kitchen, he put the milk in the refrigerator. He grabbed his freshly made sandwich, the two packets of mayonnaise that came with it, and his Dr Pepper, and headed for his couch to watch some TV, but he fell asleep before *Jeopardy* and *Wheel of Fortune*.

When he woke up, it took him a few minutes to figure out where he was. Once he realized he was home, he was able to think about what he was going to do next. First, he had to find out what time it was. Then he could take a shower, go shopping, and email Erika. That was a good plan. Who was he kidding? Everything else could wait. He couldn't wait to turn on his laptop and email Erika. He grabbed his duffle bag and took everything out. He turned his laptop on went straight for his email. But she had already written to him.

Dear Scott,

I think by the time you read this, you will probably be home. I hope you made it safely. I bet your internal clock is all over the place. You probably don't know what day it is. If you look at the corner of your computer, it will tell you the correct date and time. That is, it will if you changed it to EST, as I suggested you do before you left Afghanistan. I bet you didn't. :)

My roommate's wedding was beautiful, and everyone had a great time. Colorado is a pretty state, but I can't wait to go home. I decided to change my ticket. I'm flying home on the eighteenth instead of the twentieth. There isn't any reason for me to stay here any longer. I don't know anyone, and I am bored, so I am flying home. Besides, I remember you promising to take me out to dinner. I told you I was going to hold you to it, and I am.

Now that you are home, we can actually call each other. Here is my cell number if you feel like talking. 704-936-1547.

Glad you are home,
Erika

Scott was thrilled Erika was coming home two days early. But he was going to write her back instead of calling. He was shy when it came to girls. He had been in relationships, but he was never good about picking up the phone and calling a girl out of the blue. He wanted to call Erika but didn't want to bother her if she was busy. Then again, if she were busy, she wouldn't answer the phone. He could text her. That was almost like calling. He was overthinking again. This was ridiculous. If you can't call her, how are you going to take her out to dinner? Order through Grubhub? She could eat in her house while you eat in yours. That wasn't taking her out. That was ordering room service from two hundred miles away.

He was getting angry with himself. He flew attack helicopters for a living but couldn't call a girl. How stupid did that sound? He got his cell phone and created a contact for Erika, so he wouldn't have to remember her number, and then hit send. Her phone started ringing. One ring, two rings—if she didn't pick up by the third ring, he would hang up. On the third ring, Erika answered.

"Hi, Scott," Erika said.

"Hi," Scott said. "How did you know it was me?"

"I saw the area code, 717. That's the code for Harrisburg. You are the only person I know that lives there, so it had to be you."

"Oh, okay," Scott said. "You're right. It's me. How are you?"

"I'm doing okay. But I can't talk to you right now."

Scott felt like someone had kicked him in the stomach. He was right. She was busy and didn't have the time to talk. He shouldn't have called her. He should have emailed instead.

"I can't talk because I'm at the airport getting on a plane. I'm coming home today. One of the bridesmaids decided she wanted to stay a few more days. I changed my ticket again and took her place."

"Did you really?" Scott said.

"Yes," Erika said. "Can I call you when I land? We are boarding now."

"You bet," Scott said. "Have a good flight. Talk to you later."

Okay, that was good. Erika was coming home even earlier. They would talk later today. In the meantime, Scott would get in the shower and take care of what he needed to do that day. That way, when she did call, he would be home, and all his errands would be done.

Scott had just finished shaving when a brainstorm hit him. He was going to drive down to Arlington, meet Erika at the airport, and drive her home. He went online and found out how long the flight from Boulder to Arlington was—roughly three hours and twenty minutes if it was nonstop. Most of the flights those days had at least one stop, so that might buy him time. He also needed to know how long of a drive it was from Harrisburg to Arlington. It was two hours and five minutes. He was going to do this. He just needed to know what airline she was flying and her estimated time of arrival.

That was easy to find out. He had a good friend who worked for the FAA. Whatever information Scott needed, his buddy would tell him. With Scott's level of security, he could find out just about anything. Erika's plane was scheduled to land at Ronald Reagan National Airport at 635 p.m. It was now 3.17 p.m. He had three hours to get there. He got took a change of clothes. If he was too tired to drive home, he would stay at a hotel. He loved wearing his uniform. But nothing beat a comfortable pair of jeans, a T-shirt—or in this case, a polo shirt—and a pair of sneakers. Scott wasn't going to wear a T-shirt to meet Erika at the airport.

His only concern was his car. Although Barbara checked on the house when he was deployed, he never asked her to start his car. He wondered if the battery had died. He had put a fuel stabilizer in the gas tank, so the gas should be fine. His car was in the garage, and the battery was on a trickle charger, keeping it alive, he hoped.

He locked up the house, went to the garage, and hoped his car would start. Sure enough, it didn't. The trickle charger hadn't done what it was supposed to do. He'd been away longer than he'd originally planned, so the trickle charger hadn't lasted. Well, two years ago for Christmas Jimmy and Barbara had bought him a portable car jump starter. That worked like a charm. Before Scott knew it, he was on Interstate 83 heading to the airport.

Chapter 26
Interstate 83

Scott had forgotten how much he loved driving his new car, a Dodge Challenger. He had bought it a year and a half ago but didn't have much time to drive it because he was deployed. It was still new to him. He'd never thought he would love any other car like he loved Caroline, his 1998 Cutlass Ciera, which had two hundred and fifty six thousand miles on the clock. Caroline had thrown a rod and had to be put to rest. When Scott loved something, he named it. Whatever it was, it always had a girl's name. He called his bowling ball Beth. His favorite shotgun he shot skeet with was Ruth. When he had Caroline—get it, CARoline?—he would tell everyone he'd named her that because she was a car. Now he had to think of a good name for this car. He needed to spend more time with her, so it would come to him.

As he headed down the interstate, he passed a sign for Hershey Park. He would love to take Erika there. What more could a woman want than a park full of chocolate? For the first time in a long time, Scott found himself making plans with someone other than Jimmy. He had committed to Jimmy and his mom that he would always be there for Jimmy. He intended to keep that promise. If everything worked out with Erika, he would tell her about

Jimmy and Jimmy about her. But suppose Jimmy and Erika didn't like each other? What would Scott do? Jimmy was Scott's little brother, and Scott loved Jimmy and wanted to be the role model he needed. Scott had also started to care about Erika and wanted to get to know her better, but he didn't want to worry about whether Jimmy and Erika would like each other. What a mess that would be if they didn't. Once again, he was overthinking this, worried about things that hadn't and might not ever happen. He was borrowing trouble, and he knew it. So he stopped.

Right now, he wanted to get to the airport in time to surprise Erika. But suppose she wasn't happy to see him? Maybe she didn't like surprises. She might have made arrangements for someone else to pick her up. He was doing it again, and he stopped himself from thinking about all the things that could go wrong, instead of thinking about what could go right. She might be happy to see him. Could she have missed him as much as he had missed her?

Those thoughts were still going through his mind when he heard, "In one mile take ramp to MD-295 South/Baltimore-Washington Parkway South toward Washington."

"Thank you, GPS lady," he said. She had snapped him out of overthinking. But the only way he was going to beat his overthinking was to change his thinking. What if this wasn't a surprise meeting or a date? What if this was a mission with an objective, a timeline, and an outcome? He found himself with much more confidence. Meet Erika at the airport, take her home, then out to dinner or maybe dinner first, then home. Here he went again. According to the GPS, his arrival time would be 5.55. p.m. which gave him plenty of time to park his car, go to the terminal, and wait for her plane to land at 6.35 pm..

"Park the car?" Scott said out loud. "Where do I park the car?" Anytime he had ever been to Ronald Reagan Airport, he had flown in. He never had to think about where he and his crew were going to park the plane. Civilian life was a whole new ballgame. I'm never going to adjust to it once I retire, he thought.

"In a half mile, take ramp on right. Your destination will be on your left." Once again, the strange female voice of the GPS brought him back from the land of overthinking.

He had reached the airport. Now he needed to find out where exactly he needed to go. Taxi cabs zoomed past, cutting in front of him from the left to the exit on the right. Other drivers merged into his lane at sixty, not caring that there was a car already in the lane. Cars to his left, cars to his right, all of this was going on while he was trying to read the signs to see what parking lot he was supposed to go to. Parking lot A was international arrivals. Parking lot B was domestic departures. Holy cow, he was never going to find the sign for domestic arrivals and Southwest Airlines.

Finally he found the sign and which parking lot he had to go to. He looked at his watch. It said six fifteen p.m. All of a sudden, he was starting to panic. He didn't want to miss Erika's arrival. He parked in the first space he found. He took out his camera and took a picture of what number and color row he had parked in. No way would he ever be able to remember where he parked, especially with Erika being next to him. He rushed into the terminal. On the screen that said Arrivals, he looked for Erika's flight number, 2751. It said "at gate."

Scott was doing well so far. He hadn't missed Erika yet. Her plane was still at the gate. He had a few minutes to calm down and gather his thoughts. To his left, he saw a man carrying roses. He shook his head. He should have brought flowers for Erika, the way that man was bringing roses to his wife or girlfriend. Oh well, maybe next time. Walking towards the gate where Erika's plane was, he saw a kiosk with flowers. But the only flowers they had left were pink carnations. Carnations were pretty. Maybe she would like them. He was still walking toward baggage claim when his phone rang. It was Erika. He didn't want to sound nervous or too excited either, so he took a deep breath.

"Hello."

"Hi Scott, it's Erika. I just landed in Washington."

"How was your flight?"

"Not too bad, but I'm a little tired. I have to get my luggage and find a taxi. Can I give you a call when I get home?"

He could see her approaching the luggage carousel.

"You don't look tired." Scott said. "I like the sweater you are wearing, too. Light green looks good on you."

"Wait. How do you know what I'm wearing?"

"If you turn around and look straight ahead, you will see me."

Now the moment of truth had arrived. No turning back. He would see her reaction firsthand, and all of his questions would be answered in a matter of seconds.

She turned. She couldn't believe it. Scott was right in front of her. She ran over to him and jumped into his arms.

"What are you doing here?" Erika asked. With tears in her eyes, she hugged him.

"I wanted to see you again," Scott said. "So I made some phone calls, found out what plane you were on, and decided to surprise you."

"This was the best surprise ever. I'm so happy to see you."

Harrisburg
Emerson Elementary School
August 20

It was time for the back-to-school meetings. Within the next two days, the teachers would get their final class rosters from Eileen and have meeting after meeting with her about this year's academic expectations. Eileen Stone was still the principal. At the end of last year, the school district had moved some principals to different schools. Thankfully, that didn't happen here because along with the other teachers, Jessica really liked Eileen.

At the end of the meeting with the principal, as the teachers were leaving the staff room, Eileen asked to speak with Jessica.

"Jessica." Eileen approached her. "I have a favor to ask."

"Okay," Jessica said. "Ask away."

"We have a situation. Richard needs to take a leave of absence."

Richard Hamilton was one of the fourth-grade teachers. Students, parents, and the whole staff loved him. He was the first to help out if anyone needed anything, both in and out of school. He made people laugh and truly was a nice guy.

"Is he okay?" Jessica asked.

"He is fine," Eileen said. "His father suffered a stroke two days ago, and he flew to St. Louis to be with his family. He doesn't know how long he will be away. Rather than getting a long-term substitute until he comes back, he and I thought you might take over."

Jessica wasn't sure how she felt about taking over a class she had never taught before. But she really liked Rich and felt sorry for him and bad about what happened to his father. It brought back memories of her father and when he had gotten sick and how many people had been there for her when she needed to be with him. However, the first day of school was less than three weeks away, and she was still getting ready for her class.

"Eileen, I have all my lessons planned out until the end of October." Jessica said. "I set up my classroom, made up the seating charts. I have plans to go away with Matt next week. I can't learn a whole curriculum in less than two weeks."

Eileen stood there shaking her head while Jessica told her all the reasons she couldn't possibly be ready for the new school year.

"So, is that a yes?" Eileen asked.

"Of course it's a yes," Jessica said. "I'll figure it all out. You know me. I thrive under pressure." She would make it work to the best of her ability. Two of her friends needed her, and she would be there to help them. Since she was a little girl, Matt had instilled in her the importance of never leaving a man behind.

"That's why I asked you. I'll get in touch with Rich and let him know."

Eileen hugged her and thanked her for her commitment and for always doing her best for the school and the students.

"Oh, one more—maybe two more things," Eileen said.

"What?" Jessica said. "I'm afraid to ask."

"You won't have to move your classroom. If you want, I will ask one of the custodians to move all the books from Rich's class to your class."

"That would be great," Jessica answered. "What was the other thing?"

"I can't be one hundred percent certain, but I think Jimmy Andrews was going to be in Richard's class. So you will have him again this year along with a couple more students you know."

Jessica was happy to have Jimmy in her class again.

"Can I pick which ones I want?"

"No," Eileen said. "If you could, you would choose all the kids you had last year to be in your class this year."

"Oh no I wouldn't. I'd just choose the quiet, good kids like Jimmy."

Both women laughed and walked out of the staff room.

As Jessica was walking down the hallway, she started thinking about Jimmy and how much she'd had in common with him when she was his age. She really liked Jimmy. He was a good boy with a good heart. He was always the first kid to help her or a classmate if they needed it. She hoped he'd had a good summer, and that Scott was able to come home from Afghanistan.

The more she thought about teaching fourth grade, the more she liked the idea. It would be a challenge. She had never shied away from a challenge and wasn't about to start now. This was a good thing. It would make her grow as a teacher, and she liked that. She also realized that she would need lesson plans for her new class by the beginning of the school year, and she wouldn't have much time to get them together before her trip with Matt and Patti.

Chapter 27
Watchtower Harbor
Bicentennial Celebration
1820–2020

Established: September fifth, 1820 by Bjornson Torgrimson

History of Watchtower Harbor:

Watchtower Harbor originally was a part of the neighboring town of Harbor Hills. Harbor Hills was settled by Scandinavian fishermen in 1818. According to the Harbor Hills Historical Society, after a severe drought, it had not rained in three months. The wheat crops were dying, and so were the wild blackberries and blueberries. The early settlers were having a hard time keeping their animals alive. The night of August seventeenth, 1820, a thunderstorm rolled in over the harbor from the south. The rain was a blessing to the settlers; however, along with the thunder came lightning. It struck the ground two miles south of the tower and sparked a fire in an open field. As the wind started to blow harder, the fire got out of control. The fire tower keeper had just returned after dinner when he smelled smoke and saw the blaze off in the distance. He rang the bell, notifying the town there was an emergency. The fire brigade did its best to put out the fire but needed help, so the men and women that lived north of the fire tower started a bucket brigade. Carrying water from a nearby pond, they were able to get the fire under control and with the help of the rain, put the fire out.

A month after the fire, the community elders decided to give a one hundred dollar reward to Bjornson Torgrimson for his quick thinking, which had saved so much land and so many homes. He respectfully declined the money and instead requested that the Harbor Hills town line move to just south of the fire tower, thereby starting a new town, Watchtower Harbor. The elders agreed. A month later, Watchtower Harbor was established. It became famous for its shellfish, an important port for cargo ships on the East Coast, and a favorite seaside vacation spot.

Watchtower Harbor Bicentennial Celebration
Event Schedule

Friday, September 5

10:00: Opening Ceremony: Town Hall, Governor John T. Parker

11:00: Tall Ships Parade: Harbor

1:00: Antique Car Parade: Main Street **Grand Marshall:** Hannah Gustavson, Great Grand-Daughter of Bjornson Torgrimson

2:00: Clam and Oyster Shucking Contest: Harbor Smith's Field: Arts and Crafts, Face Painting, Games, and Rides

Saturday, September 6

10:00: Children's Parade: Main Street
    Theme: Children of Yesteryear

12:00: Hot Air Balloon Festival: Elementary School Fields
2:00: Native Fruit Pie Contest: Smith Field
5:00: Time Capsule Opening and Resealing: Town Hall
Sunday, September 7
11:00: Blessing of the Town: Unitarian Church
4:00: Closing Ceremonies: Town Hall Select Board Members
Watchtower Harbor
Late August

Sophie and Julia were excited about the bicentennial celebration. They couldn't wait to march in the children's parade. The children had to wear clothes the kids would have worn in 1820. The boys had more choices than the girls did. They could dress up as fishermen or farmers or dress as if they were in a big city, wearing knickers and a flared collar. The girls didn't have as many choices. They either dressed up as pioneer women or girls from a big city, wearing fancier dresses. Sophie and Julia choose to go as pioneer women. Their mom had ordered their dresses online from the same website she got the girls' Halloween costumes from. Their Little House on the Prairie dresses had come yesterday, and they had worn them all day then, and today, too.

When Annalise was little, her favorite show was *Little House on the Prairie*. To this day, she still watched the reruns. The girls enjoyed watching the show with their mom but preferred to be either outside or on the computer playing the word or math games they did in school. Once the girls heard there was going to be a children's parade, that was all they could think about. Now, Julia had a couple more questions she wanted to ask her mother, but she didn't know where she was.

"Mom," Julia called out, "where are you?" She made her way into the kitchen from the living room.

"I'm in the kitchen," Annalise answered, "getting the steaks ready for Daddy to put on the grill for dinner." Sean was already outside lighting the grill.

"Mom," Julia said, "I am wondering about the dresses we are going to wear in the parade."

"What about them?" Annalise asked.

"When you were little, did you wear dresses like that? Did you have electricity, or did you use lanterns like on *Little House*? You know, back in the old days?"

Annalise gave Julia a puzzled look.

"How old do you think I am?" Annalise asked.

"I don't know." Julia shrugged as she reached into the refrigerator to get the milk. "Old. Like thirty-six."

"I'm not that old."

"Oh," Julia said. "I thought you liked watching *Little House* because it reminded you of when you were a kid."

"Yes," her mother said. "It reminds me of when I was little because I watched the show then, not because I lived during the 1800s."

"How old are you?" Julia said. "Angie's mom is thirty-six, so I thought you were thirty-six, too."

Angie was Julia's friend from school. One day, she had told everyone in their class she'd overheard her mother telling someone on the phone that she was thirty-six-years-old..

"Never mind how old I am," Annalise said. "Help me bring the dishes outside and set the table. Dinner will be ready soon."

Annalise and Julia headed outside to the patio. Annalise handed Sean the plate with the steaks on them. Julia started to set the table. Sophie wanted to help.

"What about me, Mommy?" Sophie asked.

"You can go and get the napkins and the steak sauce I left on the table."

"Okay, Mommy."

Sophie got the napkins and steak sauce just like her mom had asked, and Julia set the table. Annalise had gone back into the kitchen to get the salad, the rice, and the butter. Sean finished grilling the steaks, and they all sat down for dinner.

"This has been one of the best summers of my life," Julia said.

"Mine too," Sophie said.

"Why?" asked Sean. "How is this summer better than other summers?"

"Well," Julia said, "first, I was asked to be a flower girl at Aunt Connie's wedding. I will wear a pretty dress, and I will have a new uncle."

Sophie jumped into the conversation. "I was asked to be a flower girl too."

"Daddy didn't ask you, Sophie," Julia said. "He asked me."

Sophie lifted her left shoulder, not even looking at Julia, as if to say, "I don't care. I am going to talk when I want to."

"What else, honey?" Sean said.

"I'm not afraid to jump off the floating dock at the pond any more," Julia said.

Before Julia could finish her sentence, Sophie interrupted again.

"I never was afraid," Sophie said. "Nothing scares me."

"Daddy, tell her to stop."

Sophie loved to get under Julia's skin. It was her way of getting back at Julia for bossing her around. When Sophie saw a chance to get her sister mad, she took it.

"Sophie," Sean said. "Don't interrupt your sister again."

"Okay, Daddy," Sophie said. "I won't."

"Go on, Julia," Sean said.

"I am going to be in the children's parade for the bicentennial celebration."

They were all waiting for Sophie to interrupt her sister again. She went on eating her noodles. She didn't have a care in the world.

"The best part about this summer," Julia said, "was having you home, Daddy."

Sean looked at Julia with a smile on his face and a tear in his eye.

"That was the best part of the summer for me too," Sean said, "getting to spend so much time with my family."

Chapter 28
Jimmy's House

Scott had been home for a few weeks, but he still had not seen Jimmy. After Jimmy's two weeks at summer camp, he'd spent a week with his cousin Teddy in upstate New York. Barbara's younger sister, Jennie, lived in Syracuse. She was an ecology professor at the state university. Her son Teddy was a year older than Jimmy. The cousins rarely saw each other because they lived far away. This summer, Jennie and her husband wanted to take Teddy to Niagara Falls and asked Barbara if Jimmy could go with them so the cousins could spend time together.

Jimmy still didn't know that Scott was home from his deployment. If he knew that Scott was home, he would have never wanted to go to Niagara Falls. He would have insisted on going home after camp and spending the rest of the summer with Scott. Barbara didn't want Jimmy to miss out on seeing the Falls, which were an amazing sight, one she knew Jimmy would remember for the rest of his life, so she hadn't told him Scott was back.

Scott was excited to see his younger brother. For the first time, the shoe was on the other foot. Usually, Jimmy had to wait for Scott to come home from deployment. Now, Scott had to wait for Jimmy to get back from his vacation. Scott felt like a little boy waiting for his birthday or Christmas.

Today was going to be all about the Andrews brothers. Scott left his house at 8.15. a.m. He stopped at Donny's and picked up some doughnuts, a Boston cream for Barbara, a jelly-filled (his favorite), and a bowtie doughnut (Jimmy's favorite). He got two medium cups of black coffee and a bottle of chocolate milk for Jimmy. Scott parked in his usual spot in the driveway. Barbara was outside setting up the sprinkler to water her rock garden. Between Barbara working extra hours at her shop, Barbie's Beauty Parlor, and Scott spending time with Erika, this was the first Scott had seen Barbara, too. They spoke on the phone and texted a few times a week, but that wasn't the same. He wanted to ask Barbara if she would let Jimmy go to Watchtower Harbor with him and Erika. He hadn't asked Erika if she wanted to go yet. He wanted to talk it over with Barbara first.

"Welcome home," Barbara said. "I'm so glad you are back safe and sound."

"Hey, Barbie Doll." Scott got out of his car, walked over, and hugged her.

Barbara was happy to see Scott come home from his deployments not just for Jimmy's sake but for her own, as she genuinely cared about Scott. She was technically his stepmother, which made them family, but they were also good friends. She and Scott had become close since her husband died, and Scott had taken over as both an older brother and a father figure in Jimmy's life.

"You look good. The desert agrees with you." Barbara was teasing him. "Or is it Erika that agrees with you?"

Scott looked away, trying to hide the fact that he had started to blush. He was hoping that Jimmy was going to run outside and save him from this embarrassing conversation. Scott was always so sure of himself when it came to his work. When it came to women, he was shy and bashful.

"Let's go inside," Barbara said. "I'll make a fresh pot of coffee, and you can tell me all about her."

"I stopped and got coffee and doughnuts," Scott said. "I'll get them and meet you in the kitchen."

Barbara turned on the sprinkler and headed into the house. Scott got the coffee and doughnuts but had to wait until the sprinkler went to the other side of the garden. He'd already taken one shower. He didn't need another one.

Barbara was in the kitchen getting two mugs from the cabinet. She didn't like to drink coffee from paper or Styrofoam cups and thought Scott might want to enjoy his coffee in a real cup for a change, too.

"Where's Jimmy?" Scott asked. "I thought he would have heard my car pull up the driveway and run outside."

"He came home late last night from Pittsburgh," Barbara said. "There is an ecology seminar this weekend at the university, so my sister drove Jimmy there from Syracuse."

"Did he have a good time when they went to Niagara Falls?"

"He had a great time."

"He still doesn't know I'm home?" Scott asked.

"Nope," Barbara said. "I love to see how excited he gets when he sees you."

"Me, too."

The kitchen got quiet. Barbara wanted to know more about Erika but didn't want to pry because she knew how private Scott was. However, they were family, and if this girl was important to Scott, she would be important to Barbara.

"How are things going with Erika?" Barbara finally broke the ice.

"Things are going well," Scott said. "She's a nice girl, down-to-earth, and makes me laugh."

Barbara was happy to hear that. She thought the world of Scott and knew a nice girl was out there for him. She also understood the life of a soldier and how dedicated he was to his country. Erika's father being a soldier would make things easier for Scott. He wouldn't have to explain himself if his unit was getting called up. Erika would understand.

"I'm torn," Scott said.

"About what?"

"Between Erika and Jimmy," Scott said. "They are both very important to me. Suppose they don't like each other?"

"Suppose they do," Barbara said. "If Erika is as wonderful as you say, she will like Jimmy. Don't worry about Jimmy. I will explain to him that Erika is important to you, as well."

"Before Jimmy wakes up, I wanted to ask you something. Mike's wife rented a huge house in Watchtower Harbor next week. They are having a bicentennial celebration, and he invited a bunch of us. Since I promised you a weekend spa trip with your sisters last time I was home, I thought now would be a great time for you to go, and I could take Jimmy with me, but I wanted to ask Erika, as well. And I wanted to ask you before I ask Jimmy or Erika. Would you be okay with me bringing Erika along? If you aren't okay with it, I can just take Jimmy and go somewhere else with Erika."

Scott had promised Barbara a few months ago that he was sending her and her sisters for a weekend at a spa in the Pocono Mountains. He had no clue about spa weekends and what women did there, so he'd booked them the ultra-deluxe package. They could pick and choose what they wanted to do. If they had a good time, maybe he would book a weekend with Erika, even if he'd never thought of himself as a spa kind of person.

"That's a big step, your younger brother and your girlfriend?"

"My what?" Scott said.

The heaviness of the conversation was broken when Jimmy walked into the kitchen and went to the pantry to get a box of cereal. He didn't realize Scott was there until he went to the refrigerator to get milk. As he turned away from the fridge, he saw his older brother.

"Scott!" Jimmy yelled.

He was so excited to see Scott. Jimmy had a hundred questions.

"When did you get home? Did you just get home? How long will you be home for? Did you know I went to Niagara Falls?"

"Slow down, buddy," Scott said. "I'll answer all your questions."

"Mom, did you know Scott was coming home?" Jimmy asked.

But he didn't give her a chance to answer. He didn't want an answer; he was just happy to see Scott.

"I have so much to tell you," Jimmy said. "I went up five levels on two of the games we play."

"You did, did you?" Scott said. "I'd better start playing by myself so I can catch up to you."

The boys didn't even realize that Barbara had left the kitchen. Scott had wanted to ask her more about Erika, but Barbara was gone. Outside the bay window, she was moving the sprinkler from the rock garden to the middle of the yard. How would Jimmy take the news about Erika? Scott wanted to ask Erika to go with them to Watchtower Harbor, but he wanted to talk more to Barbara about it first. He wasn't sure whether he wanted her opinion or moral support. When Barbara walked into the kitchen, she looked like a wet cat.

"What happened to you?" Scott asked. "You do know that if you wanted to take a shower, most people do that inside the house, not in the front yard."

Jimmy started laughing.

"Oh, you're funny," Barbara said. "I didn't realize the hose got kinked. I went to unkink it, and the sprinkler went crazy and got me all wet."

"More like soaked, Mom," Jimmy said.

"Never mind, young man," she said to Jimmy.

To Scott, she said, "He got his sense of humor from you."

"I'm afraid he did," Scott answered.

He loved that he and Jimmy had so many traits in common. But sharing the same sense of humor was by far the best.

"Hey, Jimmy," Scott said. "Why don't you go downstairs and set up the games so I can talk to your mom for a minute?"

"Okay." Jimmy left the kitchen and went downstairs.

"Well," Scott said. "What do you think?"

"If Jimmy wants to go, yes," she said. "I have no doubt everything is going to go well. However, if something doesn't go right, don't call me. My phone will be off. I will be at the spa getting pampered."

With that, Barbara left the kitchen and headed to her room to change into dry clothes. As she was leaving, she told Scott to go downstairs and talk to Jimmy. Scott sat down next to him on the couch and grabbed the controller off the table.

"Hey, buddy," Scott said. "Before we start playing, I want to ask you a question."

"Okay," Jimmy said.

"You remember Colonel Cullen?"

"Yeah, I like him."

"He likes you too, buddy. He rented a house for a week; he invited me and wanted to know if you wanted to come with me."

"Really? Me, too?"

"Yes, you too," Scott said. "Your mom says it's okay for you to go. Do you think you would want to?"

"Yes!" Jimmy said. "Where is this place, anyway?"

"It's an eight-hour drive from here."

"Near Niagara Falls?" Jimmy asked. "That's about eight hours, I think."

"No," Scott said. "It's on the opposite side. It's in New England."

"Oh, like where the Pilgrims are from," Jimmy said. "We learned about that this year in history."

"Around that area," Scott said.

Scott was fiddling with the controller and the wire. He was biding his time, trying to figure out how to tell Jimmy about Erika.

"Hey, buddy," Scott said, "before we play games, I wanted to talk to you about something."

"Okay," Jimmy said.

"I might ask a friend to go with us," Scott said. "Her name is Erika."

"Is she your girlfriend?" Jimmy asked. "I don't think you've ever had one of those before."

Scott had to laugh. Not that Jimmy was right, but it had been a while since he'd had someone in his life.

"She is kind of like my girlfriend," Scott said. "You know how important you are to me. I want you to meet her and tell me if you like her."

"Is she bossy?" he asked. "Girls can be bossy. The girls in my class were bossy. I didn't like them. Mom can be bossy, too."

"Erika is very nice, and she is funny," Scott said. "I don't think she is bossy."

"Sometimes girls can be nice at first. Then they become bossy."

Scott laughed. Jimmy knew more about girls than he did.

"You might be right," Scott replied.

"Will she let you play video games with me?"

"Jimmy," Scott said, his tone getting serious, "the only thing that will come between you and me playing video games is my job."

"Can we play now?" Jimmy asked. "I have to show you how good I am."

"You bet."

Scott's House

Later that same day

Scott always had a wonderful time with Jimmy and Barbara. He couldn't believe how much and how fast Jimmy had grown since his deployment. That made his decision to put in for a desk job that much easier. Although Erika was an important person in his life, his decision was about what was best for Jimmy, teaching him how to grow up to be a good man.

He looked at his watch. It was eight thirty p.m. He wanted to talk to Erika before it got too late. She had to wake up early for work tomorrow. He sent her a text asking her if she felt like FaceTiming or just calling. She said FaceTime. He brushed his hair. He wanted to look his best, and he was sure she did the same because she always looked perfect as far as he was concerned.

He called her on FaceTime, and there she was.

"Hello, beautiful," he said when she answered.

"How was your day with Jimmy?"

"A lot of fun," he said. "He is growing up way too fast."

"I can tell you had fun," she said. "You look happy."

Did she think it was just spending time with Jimmy that made him happy? Seeing her made him happy, too.

"What's wrong?" she asked. "Your face went from happy to concerned in one fell swoop."

Scott didn't realize that his face had changed that quickly. He didn't mean for that to happen.

"Nothing is wrong," Scott said. "I wanted to ask you a question, but you don't have to answer it right away."

He was so anxious about having this conversation with her. Would she want to go away with him and Jimmy? Suppose she didn't like kids at all? Maybe, as usual, he was stressing out over nothing. He wished he could be as confident in all areas of his life as he was in his job.

"Okay," she said, "ask away, but don't look so serious."

"Okay, I won't, or I will try not to. Here goes. Mike, my colonel, and his wife are renting a home in Watchtower Harbor next week. The town is having a bicentennial celebration, and he has invited our unit to join him. I wanted to ask you if you would like to come with me. Before you answer, Mike also wanted me to bring Jimmy.

It's okay if you say no, but I really would like you to come and spend some time with Jimmy and me."

"You, me, and Jimmy?" Erika asked.

Scott's heart sank. He should have known it was too soon to ask her to go away and bring Jimmy.

"I think spending time with you and Jimmy would be a lot of fun."

"So, that's a yes?" Scott asked.

"Yes, silly. It's a yes."

Scott sank back on his couch and exhaled a huge sigh of relief. Maybe this would work out better than he was thinking. He sure hoped it would.

Chapter 29
Jessica's House
September 1

Matt left his house in Washington, D.C., a day early to get to Jessica's house on Wednesday instead of Thursday. If he got to his sister's house a day early, his wife, Patti, and Jessica could gossip or whatever women did that whole day and night. Maybe, just maybe, if they stayed up all night talking, the seven-hour ride to Watchtower Harbor wouldn't seem like a seventeen-hour ride, because their jaws would be tired and they would sleep most of the way.

He loved that his sister and wife got along so well. They were the two most important women in his life. But when they got together, it sounded like feeding time at the chicken coop. As Matt and Patti turned into Jessica's driveway, Jessica was in her front yard watering her flowers. It took thirty seconds for the two women to start chatting. He hadn't put the car in park before Patti said hello from the car window. Nothing was going to stop them from talking, not even a moving car.

"You two are like two clucking hens," Matt said. "Cluck, cluck, cluck. You don't stop talking long enough to catch your breath."

"If we are clucking hens," Jessica asked, "does that mean you are an old goat?"

She walked over to the driver's side of the car and hugged her brother.

"Baaaaad joke," Matt said. "I'm going to head into the house and get your suitcases and put them in the car, so maybe we can leave on time tomorrow."

"Good idea," Jessica said. "That will give us girls time to talk about you."

"Then I'm going to gas up the car, grab a cup of coffee, and pour it over my head."

Just as he suspected, neither woman was paying attention. They hadn't heard a word he'd said. Inside, as Matt went down the tiled hallway to Jessica's bedroom, he hoped against all odds that his sister remembered to pack lightly. They were only going away for the weekend, so she shouldn't need more than two bags. She tended to overpack and brings things she would never use. Once, a few years ago, she had visited them and packed an electric converter, a necessity when going overseas but not when traveling within the United States. That was Jessica. He loved his little sister, so he didn't care. He just liked to tease her. In her bedroom were two bags. He was happy… until he picked up his sister's two-ton suitcase and five-hundred-pound duffle bag. Some things never changed. He shook his head and smiled. It didn't matter. He loved his little sister.

***

Same Day
Jimmy's House

Scott had told Barbara that he was going to pick Jimmy up at noon. As he pulled into the driveway, Barbara was setting up the sprinkler to water the lawn and the flowers in the garden. Every time Scott came over, Barbara was watering something. If it wasn't the lawn, it was her rock garden with the daisies in it. He couldn't believe how many different kinds of daisies there were—purple, white, yellow, pink with white, white with yellow.

"At it again?" Scott said. "Every time I see you, you are watering something."

"Be careful," she said. "I might turn the sprinkler around and water you."

That was one of the many things he liked about Barbara. Not only was she a great mom, she had a sense of humor. He loved their banter. She always had a ready comeback.

"Your daisies are really pretty," he said. "How mad would you be if I came by one afternoon and picked some for Erika?"

"You really want to find out?"

Scott shrugged. "Maybe."

"I'll tell you what," she said. "If you can tell me which daisy is the black-eyed Susan, I'll pick a bunch for you to give to Erika."

He remembered, from when she was trying to teach him the different names of the daisies last spring, that the black-eyed Susan had black in the middle.

"That's easy," he said. "It's the purple one over there next to the white one."

She smiled, shaking her head. "You couldn't tell a black-eyed Susan from a lazy Susan."

"Next time, plant sunflowers," he said.

"No flowers for Erika, not from you anyway. I will give them to Jimmy to give to her."

They both started laughing as they walked on the stone path that led to the backyard and the patio. Her backyard looked as nice and well-manicured as the front did.

"I made lemonade this morning," Barbara said. "Would you like some?"

"Sounds good. I'll open the umbrella so we could sit at the table with some shade."

Scott looked for the handle of the umbrella so he could start to open it. Barbara walked outside with a glass pitcher with lemons on it and three matching glasses on a plastic tray that matched the glasses and the pitcher. That was Barbara's thing. Everything had to match. Even the placemats had lemons on them. As she was pouring the lemonade, Jimmy came outside.

"Hey, buddy," Scott said. "Ready to go?"

"I am now," Jimmy said. "Mom said I had to clean my room and make my bed before we left."

"What about you, Barb?" Scott asked. "Are you ready to go?"

"I'm all set," she said. "Just waiting for my sisters to get here tonight, and off we go in the morning."

"We'd better be going," Scott said to Jimmy. "We'll stop and get something to eat on the way to my house."

"I'm in the mood for pizza," Jimmy said, "in case you were wondering."

"I wasn't really wondering," Scott said. "Take your glass inside and get your bags."

Jimmy took his glass into the kitchen and put it in the sink. He ran upstairs and got his bags. Scott gathered the other glasses and pitcher and took them inside.

"Just put everything on the table," Barbara said. "I'll wash them in a minute."

"I can wash them," Scott said.

"Thanks, but you have to be getting home," Barbara said. "I'm sure Erika is on her way."

"She is," he said. "She should be here by three if she doesn't hit traffic."

A few months ago, Scott never would have imagined meeting Erika and taking her and Jimmy away to not just any place, like the Jersey Shore, but a really nice place. Sure, for a quick getaway, he liked the Jersey Shore. He had taken Jimmy there almost every summer since he was little. But this weekend's getaway was different, and that shook Scott down to his bones. He was bringing his friend, a girl, but not his girlfriend—or was she? They'd never discussed it, so he wasn't sure what they were to each other. Well, at the moment, he wasn't going to try to define their relationship. He only knew he was bringing her to meet his commanding officer, Mike's wife, and the families of the men he worked with.

Jimmy had his suitcase in one hand and his Nintendo Switch in the other.

Scott had been hoping Jimmy might not bring his Switch or any other video equipment. But Jimmy was still young, and he would be with a bunch of grown-ups, so in the grand scheme of things, it was probably good for him to bring it.

"Give your mom a hug," Scott said. "We need to get going."

Scott hugged Barbara as well, and they headed out the door.

Scott's house

The closer it got to three p.m., the more nervous Scott was. Jimmy and Erika were going to meet for the first time. Scott went outside and sat on the deck. He didn't want Jimmy to see him jittery and crazy. Questions ran through his head on a conveyer belt. Suppose she didn't like Jimmy? Suppose Jimmy didn't like Erika.? Then what? Suppose Jimmy wanted to play a video game with Scott. He couldn't leave Erika alone and go off and play. Suppose Erika wanted to watch a cheesy girly movie. Jimmy wasn't going to want that?

"Brace yourself," Scott said to himself. "You fly Apache helicopters for a living, and this is making you nervous?" *Terrific, now I'm talking to myself.* He wished he was back in Afghanistan. He knew what to do in combat. Hoping Jimmy and Erika get along was making him crazy. But they were both so important to him, and if they didn't get along, what was he going to do?

"Scott," Jimmy yelled out. "Where are you?"

"I'm out on the deck, buddy."

"I think Erika just pulled up on the driveway."

The moment of truth was here. As he stood up from the lounge chair, his foot got caught on the chair's leg, and he almost fell on his face. Luckily he caught himself and fell onto the other chair. He took a deep breath and went inside. By the time he reached the front door, Jimmy had opened it, and he was waiting for Erika to walk up the stairs.

"You must be Jimmy."

"Hi, Miss Erika." Jimmy extended his hand.

"You are such a gentleman," she said.

"Thank you, ma'am. Scott told me never to call a lady by her first name without putting 'Miss' in front of it."

"You taught him well," Erika said to Scott. The wind blew her long brown hair away from her face, making her smile brighter than the sun. He tried to go to her, but it felt as if his feet had melted into the pavement. She walked over and gave him a big hug.

"I'm trying," Scott said. "How was the drive up?"

"Not too much traffic at all."

Scott took Erika by the hand, and they walked into the house and sat on the couch in the living room. Jimmy followed, picking up the Switch that was charging on the table. Scott was hoping that Jimmy would leave it alone for a little while so he and Erika could get to know each other.

"Is that your Switch?" Erika asked. "I brought mine. I was hoping we could play together."

"You have a Switch?" Jimmy asked.

His face lit up like a candle. He couldn't believe an adult had a Switch. And she was a girl, too!

"I sure do," she said.

"Do you ever play multiplayer?"

"Sometimes," she said. "I brought Rocket League, Mario Kart, and Overcooked. We can play my games or yours."

Scott got up from the couch and headed into the kitchen to put on a pot of coffee. As he entered the kitchen, he looked back at Jimmy and Erika. "Wow," he said to himself, "she is good. And to think I was worried."

Chapter 30
Watchtower Harbor
Labor Day Weekend

The parade was two days away. Tourists of all ages from nine months to ninety crowded the streets of Watchtower Harbor. The townspeople were still hard at work, putting up banners on the overpasses outside town, painting the parade routes, building games booths, and getting the Town Hall ready for the local state and town officials.

The girls were so excited. All the rehearsing they had done every day for the past week was going to pay off. They were nervous because they were on the lead float starting off the parade.

Their float wasn't the kind you would see on TV at the Macy's Thanksgiving Day Parade with helium balloons of Snoopy the Astronaut, Spiderman, or Hello Kitty. The girls would be walking beside a float made from an antique tractor usually on display in the Watchtower Historical Society Museum. The Hoskinns family owned it. Adam Hoskinns's family roots could be traced back to 1720, almost one hundred years before the town was settled. The Historical Society had asked to borrow his family's tractor because Adam was the great-grandson of Jeremiah Finlay, a fisherman, farmer, and the town's first solicitor.

Even the use of antique tractors came with its drama. One of the museum's curators, Mandy Roberts, a bitter, cantankerous woman, had promised her son he could drive the tractor. Adam Hoskinns was not going to stand for that. Either he drove it or it was not going to be in the parade.

The girls couldn't believe that Mr Hoskinns's and Ms Roberts's disagreement had turned into a huge argument in front of everyone marching in the parade. The girls didn't care for Ms Roberts. She was a horrible woman who never smiled and was always in a bad mood. Years ago, rumor had it, she had run for a position in the Town Hall and only received one vote, hers. Was that true? Well, it made sense because no one liked her. Today after rehearsal, the girls couldn't wait to tell their parents about how Ms Roberts almost ruined the parade.

"Mommy," Julia yelled as she ran through the front door.

"Slow down, Julia," Sean said. "I don't want you to trip. Your mom is at the farmers' market."

"Hi Daddy," Julia said. "I can't slow down. So much happened at rehearsal today. Ms Roberts almost ruined everything. She is so mean. She wasn't going to let Mr Hoskinns drive the tractor in the parade. She promised her son he could drive it. Mr Hoskinns said, 'No way. This belongs to my family. I take care of it. I am going to be the only one who is going to drive it.'"

"Well, Mr Hoskinns does have a good point," Sean said. "It does belong to his family, and Ms Roberts is just going to have to understand that."

Sean was trying not to express how he felt about Ms Roberts. Sean didn't care for her either. She was a sour woman.

"How about you, Sophie?" Sean asked. "How did rehearsal go for you?"

Sophie was more interested in getting something to drink out of the refrigerator than what happened with Ms Roberts.

"It went fine," Sophie said. "I am a little scared about starting the parade. We are the very first in line."

"You have nothing to worry about, sweetheart," Sean said. "Your mom and I will be there cheering on the two most beautiful little farm girls in the parade."

Sophie was pouring herself a cup of milk and shaking her head, the way she had seen her mother do hundreds of times when talking to her father. "Mommy is right about you, Daddy."

"Oh yeah, right about what?" Sean asked.

"You are impossible."

Sean laughed. Sophie was right. Annalise said that about him daily. Sophie was drinking her milk out of her favorite princess cup. Julia was over by the pantry looking for a snack. He loved his family so much and loved having spent the entire summer with them. He wanted to stay forever. However, he had received his orders, and he was leaving again. He was struggling with how to tell them. He would have to go in the middle of the night. Though he didn't know the date, he would have to be at the base by 0400. The disappointment on his girls' faces always tore him apart. Now, as they were getting older, leaving them was becoming harder and harder.

Jessica

Jessica never seemed to have a dull moment in her life, not at home, and not in the classroom, either, but now she was on vacation, so she was going to relax and enjoy it. Matt drove up the crushed-shell driveway to the two-bedroom cottage he had rented for the weekend. The cottage was just as she had imagined. It had a freshly painted white picket fence with purple and white hydrangeas poking through the slats. Above the white wicker rocking chairs, the porch was lined with hanging baskets of double blooming pink geraniums. Miraculously, everything was the same as she remembered when she and Matt vacationed in Watchtower Harbor with their parents many years ago.

Scott

Once again, the moment of truth had come for Scott. They were getting close to the house Mike and Gail had rented. How was he going to introduce Erika to his other family? If he'd been nervous introducing Erika to Jimmy, introducing her to Mike and his wife was throwing him into a state of panic. They might have to call the ambulance, give him oxygen or have him sedated. Scott's crew were like his family. He always wanted everyone to like each other.

But he wasn't concerned with the other members of his unit as much as he was with Mike. Scott looked up to

Mike and respected him as much, if not more, than Scott had respected his own father. Mike's opinion mattered. Of course, the relationship between him and Erika was just that, between the two of them.

"Okay, dude," Scott said to himself. "You were worried about how Jimmy and Erika were going to get along. That went great. This is going to go even better than that. Holy cow! Combat is so much easier than this. You go, do your job, and come back."

According to the GPS lady, the turn-off for Sea Captain Way was coming up in five hundred feet. Scott was still a million miles away. He would have missed the turn-off if the GPS lady hadn't repeated, "Turn right onto Sea Captain Way."

"There is number eighteen on the right," Erika said.

The driveway had to be a quarter of a mile long. It was lined with Leyland cypress trees that were thirty feet tall. At the edge of the driveway were beautiful rosebushes still full of pink roses late in the season.

"Is this a driveway or a runway?" Scott said. "There better be a gas station somewhere on these grounds because we will need to fill up just to leave."

They pulled up in front of a magnificent old sea captain's house with beautiful Greek columns and a widow's walk. One couldn't help but be in awe of this house.

As wonderful as it was, Erika felt like something wasn't right with Scott. Even though he'd just made a joke about the driveway, he didn't seem like himself.

"Scott," she said. "Are you okay? Your body is here, but your thoughts are a million miles away."

"What?" he answered. "Oh yeah, I'm fine. I'm just looking at this amazing place."

His nervousness had gotten the better of him, and Erika had picked up on it. He needed to calm down, or he was going to make a mess of this whole weekend.

Only one other car was in the driveway, Mike's black 1959 convertible Corvette with red leather seats, chrome fenders, and the smallest rearview mirror ever made mounted on the dashboard because the windshield was too small to put it there.

Scott parked next to Mike's prized possession. He parked close enough to leave space for other cars but far enough away he wouldn't hit it with his car door. He'd parked close on purpose. As he was opening his door, he heard a loud bellowing sound. Mike was going to say something. Maybe it would help break the tension Scott had built up in his mind.

"Do you think you could have parked any closer?" Mike said.

"Want me to try?" Scott said.

"No, wise guy, I don't want you to try," Mike said.

The two men laughed, shook hands, and hugged each other. They were best friends and true brothers-in-arms.

Jimmy ran over to Mike, shook his hand, and hugged him as well.

"Thank you for inviting me, sir," Jimmy said. "I'm glad you came home safely,"

"You're very welcome, son," Mike said. "I'm glad we all came home safely."

Erika made her way over to Scott with a big smile on her face. She loved seeing all the interactions between Mike, Scott, and Jimmy. She was the daughter of a colonel. She understood the relationship soldiers had with each other and with their family members.

"You must be Erika," Mike said. "Scott tried to keep you a secret, until the day he left the chat window open on my computer."

Scott turned beet-red with embarrassment.

"Oh, that's wonderful!" Erika asked Scott, "Did you give secrets to the enemy as well?"

"That's a good question," Mike said. "Oh, this is fun. Now I have a partner in crime to kid you as much as I do."

"You sure do," Erika said.

"I am going to take Erika in to meet Gail," Mike said. "You can bring in the suitcases."

Scott's nervousness went away. Once again, everything was going to be fine. Erika and Mike were getting along, even if it was at his expense. He didn't care that they were teasing him. Camaraderie like that was what families did.

Chapter 31
Mike and Gail's Rental Home
September 5

Scott woke up extra early that morning. Today was going to be a busy day. The opening ceremony for the centennial celebration was at 1000, the parade of tall ships at 1100, followed by the antique car show at 1400.

Back in August, when Mike was planning this weekend with Gail, he had one request of his men. They called it an order. He called it an uncompromising request he suggested they follow. He wanted to have one sit-down meal with his men and their families. Scott loved to cook and saw the dinner as an opportunity to show off his kitchen skills, so he volunteered to prepare dinner that night. He made the best ribs in the world. At least that's what he'd bragged to his crew when they were deployed. Now it was time to put his money where his mouth was. He would need time to get the ribs and the smoker ready. He had learned how to smoke the ribs from a chef at his favorite restaurant, Smokin Hot in Georgia. It was his favorite stop in Georgia when he had to fly to Fort Benning to pick up supplies or for a meeting.

Scott was going to start smoking the ribs around 0900. By the time they came home from the festivities, the ribs would be done. He didn't want Erika or Jimmy to miss the opening ceremonies, and Scott wanted to see them, too. They would have to head into town early enough to find a place to park. Luckily the pier and the center of town were close to each other, so wherever they parked, they weren't going to have to walk much. Besides, they could scope out where they might want to sit to watch the antique car parade and the children's parade tomorrow.

More than anything, they wanted to see the tall ships today and the hot air balloons tomorrow. Tomorrow, they would be able to see the balloons from anywhere, so they wouldn't have to worry about where they were going to park. They would just have to look up to the sky. Today, they took a chance and drove down to the harbor to park the car. Scott had stopped in the middle of the road to look at the tall ships anchored in the harbor. He didn't realize he was holding up traffic until a police officer walked over to the car and told him to move along. No luck at finding a parking space at the harbor, so they drove up one of the side streets to head into town, and someone was leaving. Scott pulled right in.

"Aren't you the lucky one," Erika said. "You turn the corner and you find a spot."

"Jimmy," Scott said, "what do I always say?"

"I'd rather be lucky than good," Jimmy said.

"One hundred percent correct," Scott said. "Because it's so true."

Erika shook her head and smiled at him. They headed to the pier. As they walked down the sidewalk, they could see the ships between the houses they were passing. Jimmy was amazed at how tall the ships were. He was describing them to Scott and Erika as if they weren't there to see them for themselves.

"Did you see that one?" Jimmy said. "They call that a windjammer. It must have fifty sails. It has to have that many because it doesn't have an engine. If the wind isn't blowing, the ship isn't moving."

"How would you like to climb up one of those masts to fix one of the sails?" Scott said to him.

"No way, not me," Jimmy said. "I would be the captain on that ship. If I didn't like someone, that would be his job."

Scott and Erika laughed. The parade was about to start. They looked for a place on the pier to sit, but again, no luck. But the tide was going out, and a few people were already sitting on the jetty. The rocks wouldn't be the most comfortable place to sit, but you couldn't beat the view, and since the tide was going out, they weren't going to get wet either.

Friday Evening
Dinnertime at Mike's house
1800

Badger and his girlfriend, Stacy, were the last ones to arrive. They had gotten stuck in traffic crossing the bridge.

"Hail, hail, the gang is all here," Mike said. "About time you showed up. We were going to start without you."

"I knew I would hear about it," Badger answered. "Traffic was a nightmare."

Mike took the chicken legs and the bratwurst off of the grill and handed the platter to Badger.

"Oh, by the way, Badger, since you were the last one to show up," Mike said, "you're cleaning up."

"I'm used to cleaning up all your messes, sir," Badger answered, with a sly smile.

Everyone at the table laughed, even Mike. They had never heard Badger answer Mike like that. He was always respectful and did things by the book, so it took everyone by surprise. It set a good tone for dinner.

It was 2000. They'd put all the food away. The dishes were in the dishwasher, and the table was clean. Scott and Erika, Badger and Stacy, and Mike and Gail were sitting around the fire pit talking. Jimmy was sitting by the patio alone. He had fallen asleep while playing one of his games. He'd had a big day, and it had started early. Scott walked over to him, picked him up, got him in the house, and put him to bed. Scott headed back outside to the fire pit. Gail and Erika were talking about how quiet it was and how they could hear the waves from the ocean as the tide was coming in. Mike had also fallen asleep on the Adirondack chair.

"Well, I guess I am in for an exciting evening," Gail said. "Why don't you take Erika for a ride by the ocean?"

"What about Jimmy?" Scott said. "Should I waken him up and bring him with us?"

"Wake him up?" Gail said. "He's fine. He is sleeping. What are you worried about?

Go and have some fun. Don't stay home with us old people."

"Okay, we will," Scott said. "Thank you."

Scott didn't usually leave Jimmy alone, but he trusted Gail and knew nothing would happen. He and Erika got into his car and headed to the ocean. The full moon lit the night sky. Scott turned off the headlights for a few seconds to show Erika how bright the moon was. There were too many lights in Harrisburg at night to truly appreciate all the stars and how much light the moon gave off. They drove to the edge of the parking lot where the walkway down to the beach started. The waves were high and coming in fast, and the moon reflected off the water like a tunnel of light leading to a mystical place beyond the horizon. A few families were sitting around bonfires roasting marshmallows and enjoying the night.

"What a beautiful night," Erika said. "I'm thrilled you asked me to come here with you and Jimmy."

"I'm happy you said yes," Scott said. "How about we go for a walk on the beach?"

"Now?"

"Yes, now."

"Okay."

They got out of the car. Scott took Erika's hand, and they headed down the dunes and walk on the moonlit beach.

Chapter 32
Centennial Parade Day

What had once been months away was finally here. The townspeople and tourists had started to gather in the center of town, finding seats along the parade route. Some people were sitting on the curb while others brought lawn chairs and set them up on the sidewalks. Others were sitting on the front lawns of the homes in town. The governor, town officials, and Grand Marshall Hannah Gustavson, the great-granddaughter of Bjornson Torgrimson, were already sitting in the grandstand outside Town Hall.

Sean, Annalise, and the girls walked down to the pier from their house. It was only a ten-minute walk. The police had put up no-parking signs all over the center of town, so parking wasn't allowed at the pier, not even for people in the parade. They walked the girls to the pier. Sean could tell they were nervous about leading off the parade, but he knew they would be fine.

"Girls," Sean said. "Mommy and I have to go and find seats along the route."

"Are you sure we look nice?" Julia said.

"You are the most beautiful girls on the planet," Sean said.

Annalise and Sean gave the girls hugs and kisses and made their way along the parade route.

Harbormaster Arthur Harrison also doubled as organizer for the parade at the pier. He had to make sure each marcher and each float left at its assigned time. Fishing boats were coming in to unload what they had caught, and boat owners wanted to go out to do a little cod fishing and escape the craziness of the day's festivities. It was 0900, show time, and Arthur was going to make sure nothing went wrong. Everyone was lined up and ready to go. He gave Steven Leon, the leader of the color guard, the go-ahead, and the parade started.

Jessica, Matt, and Patti woke up extra early. They wanted to sit in the same spots they had when they were kids on vacation. Back then, they sat on the sidewalk across the street from the general store to watch the Fourth of July parade. After the parade they would go into the general store and buy stick candy. Matt would get root beer and Jessica would get orange. They wanted to know if Nick was still there and if he was still giving kids pieces of saltwater taffy. It was a long time since they had been to Watchtower Harbor. They wanted to recreate everything they did when they were younger and share their memories with Patti. Last night they'd had dinner at the pier, and they had played miniature golf. Today, the parade would go to a beach for one of the four bonfires the town was having. When they were little, they'd always had one day when they didn't plan anything. Tomorrow was going to be that day. Maybe they would go to the drive-in and watch a double feature. Not many places had drive-in movie theaters any more. Most of them were probably torn down and replaced by strip malls. Matt and Jessica hadn't been sure Watchtower Harbor's theater, which had opened in 1957, would still be there, but sure enough, when they drove past last night, they saw that its sign was still up.

They were having fun watching the floats go by. One sponsored by the local shell fishermen had just passed. The float had huge plastic oysters that opened and closed, each at a different interval. Sitting inside them were girls dressed up like mermaids holding pearls.

Directly across the street from Matt was someone he thought he knew from when he was younger. It couldn't be. She had been a little girl then. Now, she had grown up, and he was older, but her face hadn't changed, and he would never forget what she looked like.

"Matt," Patti said. "Are you okay? You look like you've seen a ghost."

"What?" he said. "Yeah, I'm okay. See that woman across the street with blonde hair in the light blue shirt. She looks familiar, but I can't figure out who she is."

Matt knew who she reminded him of, but no way was he going to bring up that memory. It was too crazy and farfetched.

"An old girlfriend." Patti was teasing him.

"Maybe that's it." Matt teased her right back. He was trying to play it off and not let it seem like he was losing his mind.

He tried to shake the blonde woman off, but she looked so much like Annalise, the girl who had showed up in his dreams many, many years ago when he was deployed to Bosnia. The dream was so vivid, he still remembered it. She had told him that Jessica missed him and wanted a letter or a phone call. Matt had never told anyone about that dream, not even Jessica. Now, for the first time in a long time, he wondered if it had actually been a dream.

The parade was just about over, and people started packing up their chairs and heading to the parking lots.

Others were still sitting in their chairs, waiting for the crowd to disappear so they wouldn't bump into anyone or have to fight their way out of the parking lots to go home. Still others headed to the restaurants to have late breakfast or possibly early lunch. That's where Matt, Jessica, and Patti were going.

At the restaurant, Matt gave the hostess his name. She handed him a pager. He headed back outside to sit with the girls until their name was called. Also waiting at the restaurant were Scott, Erika, and Jimmy. Matt thought he was going crazy. This time it was Jimmy who looked familiar. Just to make sure, he was going to ask his sister.

"Hey, Jess," Matt said. "That little boy over there with the camo shirt on, doesn't he look like one of your students?"

"Holy cow," Jessica said. "It looks like Jimmy—because it is Jimmy. That's probably Scott, too. Let's go over and say hi."

Jimmy's back was turned, so he didn't see Jessica walking up to them until he turned around.

"Ms Beck?" Jimmy said. "Is that you?"

"Of course it's me," she said.

"What are you doing here?" Jimmy said. "Shouldn't you be getting ready for school?"

"I am allowed to leave Harrisburg once in a while, you know."

"Scott," Jimmy said, "this was my teacher last year. Ms Beck was the one that told me to send a wish to the universe when I didn't hear from you, and you called me from Afghanistan. Remember?"

Before Scott could answer, the pager Patti was holding went off. Matt was intrigued by what Jimmy had said and wanted to know more. Sending a wish to the universe when he hadn't heard from Scott for a long time sounded a lot like what Annalise had told him Jessica had done.

"Won't you join us for lunch?" Matt asked Scott. "It could be another twenty minutes before you get a table. Let me ask the hostess if that would be a problem."

"We couldn't impose on your lunch," Scott said.

"It's not an imposition at all," Matt said. "You would be doing me a favor. I've been listening to these two hens clucking nonstop for the past two days. Besides, I'm older than you, which means I probably outrank you. I could make this an order."

Matt remembered that Jessica had told him Scott was in the military at the veterans' event she'd had at school.

"Yes, sir," Scott said. "You could."

The hostess and the waitress managed to add three seats to the table they had available. After they were seated, the waitress came right over and took their orders. The women were talking up a storm. The men, including Jimmy, had no idea what they were saying. They were talking so fast. Matt took the opportunity to ask Jimmy about what he'd said earlier about the universe.

"Jimmy," Matt said. "You said something earlier about the universe. I didn't quite understand. Could you tell me what you meant?"

"Yes, sir." Jimmy was very formal and knew his manners. "That's easy."

"I would like to hear the whole story myself," Scott said. "I have a couple questions, too."

"Well, one day I was in class, and Ms Beck knew I was sad because Scott was in Afghanistan and I hadn't heard from him in a long time. I was afraid he was hurt."

Jimmy caught the women's attention. They stopped talking because they wanted to hear what he was saying.

"Ms Beck told me she understood how I was feeling because when she was a kid, when you went away for a long time, she missed you and was afraid something terrible had happened."

Jessica's eyes started to well up. Even though her brother was sitting next to her with no chance of being deployed because he had a desk job at the Pentagon, the fear came rushing back as if she were ten years old again. She didn't like having those feelings then, or even remembering them now, for that matter.

"She told me that when she was really scared and missed you, she would find a quiet place and make a wish into the universe that you were okay, and that she wanted you to contact her as soon as you could. The universe would send a special messenger or an angel to give you the message. She said within a day or two, you called her. I did that with Scott, and the next day, he called me. I couldn't believe it. She said that you have to believe, and the wish must be from your heart. If it is, the universe will listen."

Matt put his arm around his sister to reassure her he wasn't going anywhere. She hated it when he was deployed. But he had always thought she would miss him because she was alone in the house with Mom and Dad. He had never realized she was afraid he could get hurt or killed.

"You used to talk to the universe because you missed me?" Matt asked her.

"Yes, I did," Jessica said. "With you gone, I had to take out the trash."

"You're funny," Matt said.

Since Matt's arm was already around her, she decided to hug him and tell him she loved him.

The waitress came to the table with a huge tray full of food. Her timing couldn't have been any better. It broke up the heaviness of the conversation. Besides, they were all starving. The women went back to talking about how they wanted to stop in a couple of the boutiques on Main Street and do a little shopping. That meant lots of money was going to be spent. Matt was unsure whether to ask Scott his next question. He was curious how Scott knew to call Jimmy. Was it a hunch, a gut feeling, or did he dream he saw someone in his tent, the way it happened with him?

"Scott," Matt said. "You're a pilot, correct?"

"I am," Scott said. "I fly Apaches."

"Many pilots I know are superstitious. Are you?"

"I have my rituals," Scott said, "stuff I do before and after a flight."

Matt didn't care whether Scott was superstitious or not. He was trying to make conversation, small talk, in hopes of finding a way to ask him about how he got the message to call Jimmy.

"Could I ask you a question?" Matt said. "Be straight up honest with me."

"Sure thing," Scott said. "Ask away."

"Getting back to what Jimmy was saying, how did you know he needed to hear from you? Was it a hunch, your gut instinct, or... did you have some kind of dream where someone told you to call him?"

Scott hesitated. Could it be that something similar had happened to Matt? Obviously, Matt had a similar experience to Scott's, and he was trying to make sense of it. If Scott could help him, he would.

"Good question," Scott said. "I'll do my best to answer for you."

Scott lowered his voice. He didn't want anyone in the restaurant to overhear him talking about night missions or anything else he'd done while he was deployed. But he wasn't going to reveal anything about the missions to Matt. He was apprehensive about telling Matt about Julia, but Scott was a good judge of character, so even though he'd just met Matt, Scott took a chance on the guy.

"My crew and I had just come back from a night mission. We had gathered a lot of information. I was dog tired."

Matt had been on night missions, and he knew how exhausting they could be.

"I think I crawled into my tent," Scott continued. "The next thing I knew, I turned over in my bunk, and I could sense someone there. When I opened my eyes, I almost jumped out of my skin. A little blonde girl with the face of an angel was standing in my tent. She told me not to be afraid, her name was Julia, and she was a special messenger. She said she brought messages from kids with family in the military who were far from home, saying they missed them, and that as soon as they could, they should call or write, so their families would know that they were okay."

Matt was hanging on every word. He couldn't believe that someone else had the same experience he did so many years ago.

"You're kidding me," Matt said. "I'm sitting here in shock. Your story has me seriously unsettled and intrigued."

Talking to Scott about all this had brought up a memory Matt had filed away. Now he remembered it as if it had happened yesterday.

Patti interrupted the men to tell them the women had finished lunch and were going shopping. "We will call you when we are done."

"You're intrigued and unsettled?" Scott asked. "Now I'm intrigued."

"I have never told anyone this," Matt said. "I didn't want anyone to think I was losing my mind and get thrown out of the Army. Something very similar happened to me when I was in Bosnia. She was blonde with a beautiful face, angelic, but her name was Annalise. Is any of this even possible?"

"Oh, it's possible. My CO had a similar dream or vision or whatever you want to call it. Julia visited him a couple of weeks after I had mine."

"Seriously?" Matt said. "Your CO?"

"Yes, sir," Scott said.

"Maybe the universe needs messengers like Julia and Annalise. When we are deployed, they let us know we are loved and missed and not alone."

"Roger that," Scott said. "Let's go and find our families."

They left the restaurant and walked down Main Street, hoping they would see someone from their group. The last thing they wanted to do was go into all of the stores looking for them. Jimmy came up with the best idea of all. He said they should sit in front of Town Hall and watch the hot air balloons, and eventually, the girls would find them.

The women were walking past Town Hall and saw the men looking up at the balloons. They had done all the shopping they wanted to for that day. They headed back home but not before making plans to meet up again at eight o'clock that night at Coombs Beach for the bonfire.

***

Sean and Annalise's house

The girls were still in their pioneer dresses. They loved them so much they didn't want to take them off. They'd had such a wonderful time marching in the parade that they started planning what they would do for next year's parade. Annalise had to remind them that there wouldn't be a celebration like this one next year because this was a bicentennial celebration. These only happen every two hundred years. The only parade the town would have was the Fourth of July parade. But the girls didn't care what kind of celebration the town was going to have. They only cared about being at the front of the line so everyone would see them first.

Sean had to tell the girls he was leaving early in the morning. He had been home since their last day of school in June. Now he had to leave before school started again. He had waited until he was certain he had to go and told Annalise that morning. She wasn't happy, but she understood. Orders were orders. Before any more time passed, he had to tell the girls.

"Girls," Sean said. "Where are you?"

"We are on the sun porch, watching TV," said Julia.

"Can you come into the kitchen for a second?"

"Be right there, Daddy," Julia answered.

Sophie got off the couch and ran into the kitchen. That way, she wouldn't have to make sure the TV or the lights were turned off. Julia would.

"Daddy," Sophie said. "Are we going to the fire at the beach tonight? All my friends will be there. Can we go?"

"Oh, the bonfire," Sean said. "Mommy might be able to take you."

"Just Mommy?" Sophie asked. "Why just Mommy? Aren't you going to come, too?"

Sean looked at Annalise sitting across the table. He could see the disappointment in her eyes. She didn't want him to leave any more than he wanted to go. He had loved being home for the entire summer with his family.

"Don't tell me," Julia said. "Not again, Daddy."

"Yes, sweetheart. I have to leave."

Seeing the look on Julia's face, he felt like someone had hit him in the stomach. It took all the air from his lungs.

"I'm so sorry, girls. It's time for me to go back to work. I'll be home as soon as I can."

"I miss you so much when you go away." Julia started to cry.

"I miss all of you when I'm gone, too. I will be home soon. I promise. You be good girls for Mommy. When I come home, we will have our fire on the beach."

One of his men was picking him up, and he needed to be ready. A car pulled into the driveway. Sean grabbed his bag, hugged Annalise and the girls, and headed out the door. The girls ran after him.

"We love you, Daddy," both girls said at the same time. Sean blew them a kiss, got into the car, and drove away. They went back into the house crying. Annalise didn't want to show them she had also been crying. With a cheery voice, she told them to change out of their dresses and meet her on the patio so they could see the hot air balloon flying over their house.

Coombs Beach

Everyone in town seemed to have decided to come to this bonfire. The town was having one at all four beaches, but everyone flocked to this one.

Erika, Scott, and Jimmy got to the beach early, to get some swimming in before everyone else in their group showed up. They also wanted to find a big enough area for Mike, Gail, Matt, Patti, and Jessica.

Annalise and the girls had just gotten to the beach. Before she got out of the car, she called Connie, her sister, and told her that Sean had left. Annalise asked Connie if she wanted to meet her and the girls at the beach. Her sister told her she and her husband would be there in ten minutes.

One of the firemen in town was in charge of the bonfire. He built a huge mound of wood. He had two starter logs, and in no time, the fire was blazing. The flames were a bright yellow, the embers glowing. It was a beautiful fire. Now it was time to make the s'mores. Children weren't allowed near the fire, so the adults there were making the s'mores and handing them out to anyone who wanted one.

As Julia was waiting to get a s'more, she saw a man who looked like Scott sitting with a group of people in front of the bonfire. She changed her mind about the s'more and ran over to her mom. She was so excited.

"Mom," Julia said in a hurried voice, "I just saw Scott."

"Scott who?" Annalise asked.

Julia asked her mother to bend down, so she could whisper in her ear who Scott was.

"You remember Scott. His little brother, Jimmy, was missing him, and I went to give him that message. He is over there with that group of people. Come with me. I have to go and see if he remembers me. I want to say hi to him and tell him I'm glad he is home."

"Are you sure it was him?"

Annalise was worried because this was the first time Julia had ever seen someone after giving them a message. Suppose it wasn't Scott but someone who looked like him. What would that man think? But Julia was so sure that it was Scott. Annalise held Julia's hand as they walked over to where Scott was sitting. He and Matt were the only ones out of the group who didn't want to go and get s'mores.

"Excuse me," Julia said. "Is your name Scott?"

Scott looked at Julia, and he froze.

"Do you know who I am?" she continued.

"Yes, I think so," Scott said. "You look like someone I know. Her name is Julia. She told me she was a messenger and came to me to tell me my little brother Jimmy missed me a lot when I was deployed."

"That's me. My name is Julia, and I am the messenger."

She hugged Scott. She was so excited to meet him. She had never met anyone she had sent messages to. She couldn't wait to introduce him to her mom.

"Mommy, I told you this was Scott. I was right," Julia said. "This is my mom, Annalise."

Matt stood up from his beach chair. His hands started shaking. He felt like he was going to pass out. All the blood ran from his face as he stared at her.

"Oh, no way," Matt said. "It can't be. You can't be the same, Annalise. Are you the same girl that came to me when I was in Bosnia all those years ago to tell me that my sister missed me?"

Annalise's eyes were welling up as she was shaking her head yes.

"Yes, Matthew," Annalise said. "I was the one that told you your sister, Jessica, was missing you."

No doubt was in Matt's mind now. She had to be the same Annalise. He hadn't mentioned Jessica's name, so how else could this woman know it?

It took a moment for Matt to compose himself and catch his breath. Once he did, he walked over to Annalise, hugged her, and thanked her for sending him that message from his sister.

"Matt," Annalise said. "We may not know it or understand it, but there is always an angel watching over the people we love that wear uniforms and serve their country."

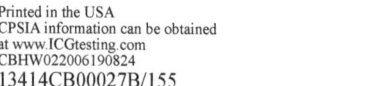
Printed in the USA
CPSIA information can be obtained
at www.ICGtesting.com
CBHW022006190824
13414CB00027B/155

9 781800 167599